IMPERATOR

GALACTIC GLADIATORS #11

ANNA HACKETT

Imperator

Published by Anna Hackett

Cover by Melody Simmons of eBookindiecovers

Edits by Tanya Saari

ISBN (ebook): 978-1-925539-54-7

ISBN (paperback): 978-1-925539-55-4

WHAT READERS ARE SAYING ABOUT ANNA'S ACTION ROMANCE

Unexplored – Romantic Book of the Year (Ruby) Novella Winner 2017

At Star's End – One of Library Journal's Best E-Original Romances for 2014

Return to Dark Earth – One of Library Journal's Best E-Original Books for 2015 and two-time SFR Galaxy Awards winner

The Phoenix Adventures – SFR Galaxy Award Winner for Most Fun New Series and "Why Isn't This a Movie?" Series

Beneath a Trojan Moon – SFR Galaxy Award Winner and RWAus Ella Award Winner

Hell Squad – Amazon Bestselling Science Fiction Romance Series and SFR Galaxy Award for best Post-Apocalypse for Readers who don't like Post-Apocalypse

The Anomaly Series – #1 Amazon Action Adventure Romance Bestseller

"Like Indiana Jones meets Star Wars. A treasure hunt with a steamy romance." – SFF Dragon, review of *Among Galactic Ruins*

"Strap in, enjoy the heat of romance and the daring of this group of space travellers!" – Di, Top 500 Amazon Reviewer, review of *At Star's End*

"Action, danger, aliens, romance – yup, it's another great book from Anna Hackett!" – Book Gannet Reviews, review of *Hell Squad: Marcus*

Sign up for my VIP mailing list and get your *free box set* containing three action-packed romances.

Visit here to get started:
www.annahackettbooks.com

CHAPTER ONE

G alen swung his sword in a massive arc, cutting down his opponent.

Swiveling, he ducked under an arm and rammed his boot into the gut of another attacker.

Pulling back, he raised his short sword, his chest heaving. Every muscle in his body burned, and his chest and head ached. He was tired. So tired.

He watched as even more fighters raced across the sand of the lawless desert arena. He stayed motionless, and waited, savoring the brief respite. He'd fight. He'd keep fighting. And he'd never give up.

The wooden stands that surrounded the arena were packed with screaming spectators. They shouted and jeered and booed in a deafening cacophony of noise. Overhead, the desert suns beat down on the floating platform that housed the arena.

Sweat dripped into Galen's right eye. He reached up, swiping it away and adjusting the eyepatch that covered his useless left eye socket. He pulled in a shuddering breath. He'd lost track of how long he'd been here at Zaabha.

Three days? Four? They hadn't let him sleep or rest. They just kept him fighting. Fighting and fighting, waiting for exhaustion to do him in.

Drakking Thraxians.

The large, horned aliens had always thrived on enslaving and hurting others. And he'd been their enemy a long time.

Galen lifted his sword another fraction and watched the fighters come. They wore ragtag clothes, and most of their faces were filled with both terror and determination. But their essences mixed in the air, hitting his senses. All Aurelians had the ability to feel a being's personality. He sensed weariness, exhaustion, and resignation. They were victims too. People snatched from their ships and planets, and forced to fight for the entertainment of sand-sucking cowards.

He saw several fighters pull ahead, coming closer. He spotted the glint of silver at their temples and his gut curdled. The Thraxians had been experimenting with implants, and it looked like they were perfecting their tech. Galen felt the pale shadows of their essences. They'd been turned from unwilling, unruly slaves into ruthless, obedient fighters.

The closest fighter—a big, green-skinned Ergite—charged at Galen with a roar. Their swords clashed. Galen swung and ducked, but he knew he was getting sluggish.

He slashed with the sword and then drove it deep.

The Ergite fell and Galen spun to face another opponent. But he was too slow. He felt the cut on his arm, but the burn just melted in with all the other aches and pains.

A giant alien stomped into view, towering over Galen. He couldn't place the species, but with shiny, bronze skin and ropes of muscle, the man was formidable.

Galen dredged up some energy and moved to kick the alien. But the alien blocked him and slammed his own blade against Galen's sword. Galen staggered back, falling on the sand.

Get up, Galen.

What did it matter? His people had gotten away. Raiden, the prince Galen had been bred to protect, was safe. The others from the House of Galen—the house he'd sweated to create and cultivate—were safe.

He saw a war axe slamming down toward him and he rolled just in time. It sliced into the sand near his head.

Fighting was what Galen knew. Honor and duty were in his blood.

So he'd fight. He pushed to his knees, and the pain made him grit his teeth. He was so *drakking* tired, and maybe he was getting too old for this.

The pitch of the crowd's shouts suddenly changed. They hammered their feet against the boards and their screams turned feverish. He spotted another fighter running toward him. The alien who was almost on him swung his head away from Galen.

A crash of swords echoed across the arena, and then Galen saw her.

She leaped into the air, flying over the heads of

several fighters. She landed, one leg out to the side, her palm touching sand.

Then she stood.

She was tall for a woman from Earth, and being the Champion of Zaabha had honed her body to strong, lean muscle.

They'd given her a ridiculous outfit, but it did show off her body. The metal corset covered her breasts but displayed a toned abdomen and arms. The leather battle skirt came to mid-thigh, and showcased her muscular legs.

She swung her sword in a flashy circle and then she charged.

She had brown hair threaded with streaks of gold, burnished by the hot Carthago suns. The strands flew out behind her as she attacked. The shattered remains of an implant were visible at her temple.

Samantha Santos sent the fighters flying. She fought her way through the group and reached Galen. Her essence hit him like a warm breeze: strong, steadfast, and threaded with steel.

"Get up, Imperator."

She had a throaty voice, and he could tell she was used to giving orders.

"Not sure I can," he replied.

Deep-brown eyes met his. "Yes, you *can.*" Her voice was firm and unyielding.

She spun, whirling fast. A new wave of implanted attackers rushed at them. Without hesitation, she launched herself at them.

As she fought, Galen managed to get himself off the sand.

Over the last few days, they'd sometimes let her in to fight with him. As an opponent reached him, swinging a staff, Galen attacked. Grunting, he drove the female fighter back, sending the staff spinning away. His gaze flicked over to watch Sam. She moved like water—strong and graceful, but with power. Watching her shook off some of his lethargy.

She was magnificent. Galen had spent decades honing and training gladiators for the Kor Magna Arena. He knew within seconds of watching a fight who would make it and who would fail, who was good and who could be great.

He watched her sword move through the air. She was sure, true, and relentless.

Galen dragged in a breath. He was Imperator of the House of Galen. A force to be reckoned with in Carthago's gleaming capital of Kor Magna. He thrust his sword at an incoming fighter, and sent the man staggering. The Thraxians, the sand suckers responsible for this abomination of an arena, were his sworn enemies.

And they were going down.

Filled with new energy, Galen strode forward. He was going to grind the Thraxians to dust beneath his boots.

He reached Sam's side, and together, they fought their way through the fighters. He kept moving his sword, trying to only wound the attackers. He could easily see that most were neither good nor skilled, just desperate.

They were forced to fight and were trapped, just like him.

He spun and found himself back-to-back with Sam. Metal clanged on metal, and then Sam rolled under his arm and cut down another fighter. But the fighters just kept coming. The marauding Thraxian ships ensured the arena had plenty of slaves. Almost all were abductees, just like Sam and the other humans who'd been taken from a space station near their home planet of Earth.

Sam took two steps and leaped into the air. Her legs scissored, her feet connecting with two more aliens, taking them down. He watched as she ran back toward him and jumped again, slashing at several other fighters.

Stunning.

"Galen."

She was still airborne, her gaze on more fighters running at them. He slapped one of his hands against the other, holding his palm up. Her sandal hit his hand, and he threw her up into the air with all his strength. She rocketed up, spun, and swung out with her legs and sword.

More fighters fell to the sand.

Sam landed and moved back to his side. A fresh wave of Zaabha attackers was incoming. He scowled, taking in more of those *drakking* silver implants embedded in the people's temples. Their blank stares left Galen's gut rolling.

These poor souls were following the Thraxians' orders, whether they wanted to or not. It sickened him.

Then, suddenly, the implanted fighters stopped their

forward charge. They stepped back, moving into a line, like soldiers in formation.

What now? His muscles tensed. He saw Sam push her sweat-dampened hair from her face, her impassive gaze narrowed on the motionless fighters.

Then the ranks broke and several large Thraxian guards strode forward.

They were big, with tough, brown skin that looked like parched desert ground. Beneath, their veins glowed gold. A set of black horns swept back off each head, and their eyes were black as darkest night.

They were all holding long stunner batons.

Drak. Right then, his rage for the Thraxians was incandescent. "Sam."

Her mouth tightened but she lowered her sword. The stun batons were pure agony.

The lead Thraxian reached Sam and wrapped an arm around her abdomen, lifting her off her feet. She struggled.

"Sam!" Galen called.

Her gaze met his just as the other Thraxian guards reached Galen. He felt a stunner jam into his lower back, and electric current rushed over him.

The intense pain made his teeth click together. He shuddered, his body crashing to the sand. Then Galen was swallowed by agony and darkness.

AT THE SOUND of the opening cell door, Sam Santos jerked awake.

She'd been dreaming of home.

She could smell her mother's cooking, hear the echo of her brothers arguing, her *papá* calling for another beer, and her young nieces giggling.

But as Sam shifted, the chain on her ankle clanked, and memories of home evaporated like mist. Opening her eyes, she stared at the dank rock walls of her cell and smelled her own sweat. Her gut clenched. She knew exactly where she was, and it wasn't her parents' cozy home in New San Francisco.

It was her own personal hell—Zaabha.

She stilled as despair tried to shove through her. She couldn't let self-pity or despondency seep in. If it did, she'd be done. She'd curl up in a ball and give up.

And Samantha Gabriela Santos did *not* give up.

She lifted a hand to the itch at her temple. She felt the jagged metal shards still embedded in her skin. Thankfully, the Thraxians hadn't tried to repair the damn thing after Galen had destroyed it. The thought of being under the Thraxians' control again, little more than an automaton, made her shudder.

She sure as hell wouldn't give the Thraxians or their allies, the Srinar, the pleasure of seeing her break. They'd already destroyed the space station where she'd worked as head of security, and killed so many innocent people.

She'd heard them talking—guards in the corridors, in the arena. They were testing the damn implants on the fighters...but they supposedly had a bigger plan for them. Her gut churned. Whatever it was, it wouldn't be good for anybody.

Movement at her cell door made her tense. Two of

the ugly Srinar guards opened the door and tossed a body onto the floor. The Srinar homeworld had suffered a plague in their past, and the survivors had fled, but had been left with huge growths and tumors that mottled their faces and skin. The door clanged shut without a word from her captors.

Sam swallowed, her gaze locked on the unmoving body lying facedown on the stone.

She took in the powerful form. Ripped leather trousers encased strong legs and he was shirtless. His bronze skin was covered in blood, and deep scratches and gashes. He'd been tortured.

Air whistled through her teeth. She could only see a bit of his battered face, and it was dominated by the black eye patch over his left eye. He had dark hair that he kept cut short, with a sophisticated-looking touch of gray at the temples.

Sam dragged herself over to him. When she pressed her fingers to his strong throat, she felt a pulse. She sucked in a relieved breath.

She pushed his hair off his face. "Galen." She stroked his temple. "Galen."

Don't leave me alone. She'd been alone here for months. She'd played the Thraxians' games in order to survive. She'd used her skills and creativity to become the Champion of Zaabha.

She'd spared the lives she could, but she'd also killed when she had to. Her chest tightened. She was no longer the responsible daughter, the smiling big sister, the fun aunt, or the dedicated security specialist.

And she knew she never would be again.

"Galen." She'd been alone until this man, along with his gladiators and her fellow surviving humans, had tried to rescue her.

She'd been alone until this man had stayed behind with her. He'd told her he was going to get her out, but now they were both prisoners.

A groan vibrated through him. Sam slid an arm under him, helping him to roll over.

She took a second to study the glorious tattoos on his arms and shoulders. They looked almost too beautiful and delicate to be on his rugged body. She also noted the scars gouged across his chest. They were red and thick, like they'd been made recently, but up close, she could see they were old. He'd been wounded badly in the past.

He was a fighter, this one.

He opened his eye, and she was struck once more by the icy-blue color.

"Sam Santos." His voice was deep and scratchy from whatever the Thraxians had done to him, but it still held a ring of authority.

She reached out and touched his stubbled jaw. She knew they'd made him fight non-stop for three days, and then they'd tortured him.

Sam knew they had to get out of there. The Thraxians would kill Galen, for sure. Hell, she was amazed he was still alive

"You with me?" she asked.

That blue eye locked on her. He managed a single nod.

"We need to get out," she said.

"Destroy... Zaabha. Destroy the Thraxians."

Her lips quirked. "Don't think you're up for that today, *mi amigo*."

He frowned, and a deep groove formed on his forehead. She was pretty sure this man was used to frowning.

"*Mi amigo*? My translator didn't translate those words."

"It's a different language from Earth. My family is Puerto Rican, and I grew up speaking Spanish and English."

"What does it mean?"

"My friend."

His eye glittered. "Are we friends, Sam?"

She helped him sit up. Damn, he was heavy. The man was all solid muscle. "Today, I'm your best friend. We've not only fought together, but now we're going to work together to get out of here."

His frown turned fierce as he fought through his pain. "Escape."

"We need to get back to the House of Galen." For a second, Sam let herself think of her friends. She knew Blaine and Harper from her security team were safe at the House of Galen, along with several other women.

"Harper and the others...they want you out of here," Galen said. "Been searching for you for a long time."

Warmth filled Sam's chest. All this time she'd felt so desperately alone, and she hadn't been alone at all.

"Take it easy there." She leaned Galen back against the rock wall.

She moved over to the small bucket of water her captors left for her. Quickly, she washed his face, scrubbing away the blood. His skin felt hot.

"You know about the Thraxian implants?" she said.

He nodded, his gaze sharpening.

"They have a plan involving them," she said.

"What plan?"

"I don't know all the details. But I know it's bigger than Zaabha."

His eye widened, then narrowed, and his gaze turned inward. He gave a small, slow nod. "For now, we focus on our escape."

"Galen, I want to ask you something." She paused for a moment. "Why did you take the humans in?" she asked. "Everyone here whispers about all the resources you've used rescuing humans."

A tiny smile tugged on his lips, and it suddenly occurred to Sam that there was some handsome under all the rugged.

"My gladiators keep falling in love with humans."

Sam splashed more water on the cloth and wiped down his neck. "Do you have someone you love back home? Someone who'll be worried about you?"

"Love isn't for me."

She looked up. "Why?"

"On my planet, I was raised as a royal bodyguard. Love was forbidden. The only attachment I was allowed was to my charge."

"Your charge?"

"The crown prince of my planet." A flash of pain crossed his face. "Raiden is my prince. Our planet, Aurelia, was destroyed by a rival planet. They'd hired Thraxian mercenaries to murder the royal family and destroy Aurelia."

Sam sucked in a shocked breath. The thought of anyone destroying an entire planet was horrifying. "I'm sorry."

"And I'm sorry you lost yours as well, Sam. Earth still exists, of course, but you have no way home."

His words were like a blow to her belly. "What?" she breathed.

"You didn't know?" His gaze traced her face. "The wormhole the Thraxians used was unstable and is gone. Even with our fastest ships, you'd be dead before you reached Earth." He exhaled softly. "I'm truly sorry."

No way home? She sank back on her knees. No way back to her family. A family she'd never see or hug again. The pain of that realization was worse than any slash from a sword. She'd never again hug her mother or smell her perfume. She'd never again elbow her brothers and tell them to quit being idiots. She'd never again snuggle up with her *papá* to watch a ballgame, or tickle her nieces.

"Sam—"

"We need to get out of here." She shoved her pain away. She couldn't deal with it right now. It was another pain she'd process at a later date.

Galen studied her for a second before he gave her a nod. Sam thought she saw a glint of respect in his eye.

"Plan?" he asked.

She eyed the door. "I'll call the guards in and tell them you're dead. We'll surprise them and take them down before they have a chance to call reinforcements. After we take them down, we run. We need to get to the lower levels and find an exit to get off this platform."

He pulled in a breath. "Not sure I can fight."

"I saw you out there, Galen. I have no doubt that the man who saved his prince, who built the most successful gladiatorial house on Carthago, and who rescued an entire group of humans, can do this."

Air whistled through Galen's teeth. He nodded and held something up. It was a shard of metal from a broken sword.

"I found this on the sand in the arena and managed to hide it."

She closed her hand around it. A weapon. It wasn't much, but it was better than nothing.

He nodded at the chain on her ankle. "What about that?"

She smiled. Reaching up, she pulled a thin sliver of metal out of her hair. It took her two seconds to pick the lock and remove the chain. "Let's do this."

She watched as he shifted back down on the floor. He might be injured, but there was a vital heat that pumped off him, and an aura of command. The Thraxians sure picked the wrong man to make their enemy.

But Sam also sensed that he was a man who held himself apart. Even in the middle of the busy House filled with his people, he wasn't one to lean or share his own needs. Sam knew because she'd been the same. Being the boss meant putting other people's needs before your own.

Galen slumped down and Sam moved to the door.

"You killed him!" She raised her voice, banging on the bars set into the door. "Galen's *dead*. You killed him."

It only took seconds before there was a thump, and the door scraped open.

She stepped back, making it look like her chain was still attached. This time, two Thraxian guards entered.

Assholes. As always, just looking at them and the golden glow beneath their dark, cracked skin made white-hot fury flow through her veins.

Rage replaced her exhaustion.

She watched one alien toe Galen with his boot, but Galen didn't move. The Thraxian went down on one knee.

"*Dios mío,* he's dead." Sam channeled some of her mother. Her *mamá* was the queen of drama when it suited her.

The aliens weren't paying her any attention as they prodded Galen. She crept closer, moving up behind the closest guard. The one that was kneeling moved to roll Galen over.

Sam launched herself at the standing guard and jammed the metal shard into the alien's back.

CHAPTER TWO

———————

As soon as Galen heard Sam attack the guard, he launched himself upward at the other Thraxian.

He caught the alien off guard and headbutted the man in the nose. The Thraxian went down with a shout, and Galen leaped on him. He landed several hard punches to the man's head.

Dazed, the Thraxian blinked up at Galen with inky black eyes burning with rage. His ugly, jagged essence hit Galen. Galen leaned over him, pressing his knees to the alien's chest. Then he gripped the Thraxian's neck and, with a quick twist, snapped it.

Galen stood and spun. Sam was still fighting with the other guard. There was gold-colored blood sliding down the alien's back and side.

Suddenly, she reached up and gripped the Thraxian's horns, then she turned and ran up the wall. She flipped, and her momentum brought the guard crashing down to his knees. She was on him in a flash, her thighs clamped around his neck. She twisted, knocking him to the floor, and followed with a hard jab to his throat.

The guard grabbed his throat, making harsh, choking sounds.

The woman did not mess around. Galen reached her, then leaned down and grabbed the bloody shard protruding from the alien's side. He yanked it out and then rammed it into the alien's neck. The Thraxian made a gurgling sound as he died.

Sam leaned down and grabbed the guards' swords and scabbards. She handed one weapon and sheath to Galen. Swallowing back the pain, he strapped the scabbard to his belt, and saw Sam sling her scabbard and belt around her waist.

She lifted her sword, testing its weight. "Let's move."

Together, they moved through the open door. The hall was empty.

Pain hit Galen and he staggered into the wall.

"Hey." Sam slid an arm around him "You've got this."

He felt the heat of her and he smelled something under the stench of blood, sweat, and grime. Something sweet and womanly.

"Let's get to the lower levels," she said.

He nodded and hobbled along beside her. "You should leave me."

"I bet you're used to giving orders," she muttered.

"I am, and used to weighing the odds. Yours are better without me."

At the end of the hall, she peered around the corner.

She urged him on. "I'm used to giving orders too. I'm used to doing things my way and I like being in charge."

Galen frowned. "As am I."

She winked at him. "This should be fun, then."

"You aren't going to leave me."

"Nope. I like a challenge." Her face turned serious. "And I never leave anyone behind. Especially not a man who sacrificed his freedom to his worst enemy to help me and save his people."

A muscle ticked in Galen's jaw. She made him sound like a hero. Old pain gnawed on him, opening up inside him like a void. If she knew the truth, she'd think differently.

"Come on," she urged. "Keep moving."

As they moved down the corridor, moans and screams echoed from the nearby cells. The sound set Galen's teeth on edge. He wanted to help free everybody, but right now, he had to focus on getting Sam out of here. After that, he'd worry about Zaabha and the Thraxians.

She led him to some stairs and they quickly moved downward. At the bottom, they rounded the corner and came upon a Thraxian guard.

The alien spun, his eyes widening. He reached for his sword.

Sam released Galen and moved fast. She launched herself at the man, and with hard, ruthless kicks and blows, she drove the Thraxian to the ground.

She'd made a name for herself in this battleground. Galen was well aware that humans were not the largest or strongest species to be found on Carthago, but clearly, she hadn't let that stop her. There was pure steel under the sleek muscles.

Sam moved back to his side again, and they crept forward. Soon the temperature began to rise, and the scent of smoke filled the air.

They came to a large, metal door. Sam wrestled with the giant latch and swung it open. A wave of heat and smoke assailed them.

They stepped inside and Galen saw it was the engine room of Zaabha.

Ahead were rows of ovens, all firing with flames and covered by thick metal grates. They were manned by dirty, tired-looking workers. As Galen and Sam entered, the workers turned to look at them, their faces blank and their eyes empty. He had no idea how long these people had been here, but he didn't need his ability to feel essences to know they'd been broken.

"Let's find the exit," Sam said. "I've heard rumors that there's an emergency exit in here."

Galen looked at the workers. "Where is the emergency exit?"

No one moved or said anything.

"Please." Sam's tone was softer. "Please tell us where it is."

Again, no one spoke, but Galen saw a young boy—a thin, scrawny teen with soot on his cheeks—move a little toward a far corner.

Galen instantly saw the wooden trapdoor set into the floor. From what he knew of Zaabha, it would lead to a metal rope ladder that could be lowered toward the ground.

All of a sudden, sirens blared, cutting through the air. Galen stiffened. *Drak.* Their escape had been discovered.

"Quick," Sam said. "We need to hurry."

Together, they strode toward the trapdoor. Sam reached down and yanked it open. Below, he saw a tunnel leading downward, with a ladder attached to one side.

Sam smiled. "Great, let's—"

There was a sudden clank of metal, and Sam leaped back with a hiss. She slammed into Galen and he caught her. A solid-metal door slammed closed over the top of the ladder, blocking the exit.

"No!" She dropped to her knees, yanking at the steel plate.

Galen could already tell it was too thick and heavy to move. "They've gone into lockdown."

Sam stood, looking out the barred windows lining the engine room. He followed her gaze. The desert lay far, far below.

Sam looked at him. "If we can't lower a ladder to the ground, then we'll have to lower Zaabha."

He blinked. "What?"

She swiveled. "First we need to bar the doors." She strode back to the large doors. She looked around and then grabbed some long metal tools that were clearly used for stoking the fires. Galen followed and grabbed some more tools. Together, they slid them through the handles.

Then Sam turned toward the closest worker. "How do you shut them off?" She gestured at the ovens powering the engines.

The older worker just stared at her. "You're the Champion of Zaabha."

"Yes. And I'm planning on destroying Zaabha and freeing everybody."

The worker looked around at the others with wild eyes.

"Impossible," an old woman bit out.

Sam pointed to Galen. "See him? That's Imperator Galen of the House of Galen. He and I are going to do it together."

A young woman stepped forward, her long hair tangled over her face. "I'll show you." She moved to the nearest oven, fiddling with some metal valves on the side. "If you shut off these valves, it snuffs out the fires."

"Thank you," Sam said.

Galen pushed off the wall and together, he and Sam moved to the closest ovens. He followed the woman's instructions, ignoring how hot the metal was, and closed the valve. Across from him, Sam did the same.

They watched the fire die down inside, then eventually go out.

Sam looked at him, and they shared a brief smile. They continued to move down the line of ovens, shutting them down.

"You'll kill us all if you crash the platform," a woman yelled.

"We aren't going to shut them all off," Galen said. "We just want to lower the platform enough for us to get off."

"Then you'll abandon us," someone else said.

Sam spun, her hands on her hips. "We can't fight Thraxians alone."

Galen stepped up beside her, his arm brushing against hers. "We need an army. We *will* be back."

"I promise," Sam said, "we will return for you."

Suddenly, the platform started to tilt beneath their feet.

Sam bumped into Galen, and he wrapped an arm around her. As he held her close, he realized she had curves that he hadn't expected—lush breasts, round hips, and a generous ass. A hidden softness that he hadn't guessed at.

The platform tilted farther and people screamed. Galen and Sam went sliding, and hit one of the barred windows.

"Galen, look," she said.

He stared outside at the huge sand dunes below. They were getting closer, but the platform was still too high up in the air for them to jump.

Suddenly, a heavy pounding sounded on the engine room doors.

"Shit!" Sam moved, crawling up the floor to stare at the doors.

There was more banging from the outside, and the doors vibrated. The metal tools they'd used to bar the doors held. For now.

But the banging increased, and they both watched as the metal doors started bending inward.

"*Drak*," Galen ground out.

"Suggestions?"

"We need to get off this platform," he said.

They both made their way back toward the windows. Most of the workers were huddled together now, fighting to keep their balance on the tilted platform.

At the window, Galen felt another wave of nauseating pain. He'd done a pretty good job of keeping it at bay, but right now, he felt like his insides were on fire.

Sucking in a breath, he grabbed the metal bars of the windows and heaved. He heaved again, and the bars began to bend. He kept working on them, listening to the banging at the doors and feeling sweat slide into his eye.

"Keep going, Galen." Sam pressed against his back, her hands coming around him to grip the bars beside him. She added her strength to his.

He heaved again.

"That's enough," she said.

Galen studied the gap and knew it would be a tight fit, but it would do. Sam climbed through the gap and out onto the ledge outside. He followed, shoving his shoulders through the opening.

The wind tore at their clothes, and a wave of dizziness washed over Galen.

Sam gripped his arm. "Hey, boss-man, stay with me."

He gritted his teeth. He'd vowed to get her out of there, and if there was one thing Galen was good at, it was keeping his vows.

Except your one to the royal family and your fellow royal guards.

Old guilt bit at him. Now certainly wasn't the time to ponder past failures. The platform tilted more, and Galen watched as several items and people spilled over the side from the arena above. A Srinar guard fell past, screaming, arms waving. A shower of sand poured over the edge.

Then came a smashing sound from inside the engine room.

Galen stiffened. The Thraxians had broken through the door.

Sam grabbed Galen's hand, fingers twining with his. "It's now or never. We jump, or we go back into a cell."

He hissed out a breath. The ground was still too far away. They'd break every bone in their bodies.

Inside, the deep, guttural shouts of the Thraxians added to the roar and groan of the yawing ship. He glanced over, and through the bars, he saw the Thraxian guards thundering in their direction.

"We are getting out of here," Sam said.

She yanked on his hand and leaped off the platform, pulling him with her.

With a curse, Galen followed her.

THEY WERE FALLING.

The wind whipped into Sam's eyes. *Dios*, they were falling fast.

The ground rushed up at them, and she knew this was going to hurt. Her hand was torn from Galen's.

She hit the dune hard and tasted sand in her mouth. She groaned, pain rocketing through her. Pulling in a breath, she rolled over. She was pretty sure she'd bruised a rib or two.

"Galen," she croaked.

A few meters away, she saw him lying facedown in the sand. He groaned.

With a gut-deep effort, she crawled over to him, grabbing him. He rolled over and wrapped an arm around her, pulling her to his chest. Together, they lay there, trying to pull themselves together.

A shadow passed over them and they both looked up.

Sam sucked in a breath. The Zaabha platform flew directly overhead. She watched as it slowly righted itself, and kept going.

"It's not stopping." *Dios mío*. She squeezed her eyes closed and gripped Galen. "It's gone."

She was free.

For the first time in months, she wasn't trapped at Zaabha. She wasn't on the arena sand, forced to fight to the death.

Beneath her, the desert sand was hot, and above her, Carthago's dual suns were bright in the sky. And beside her, Galen was a hard, steady presence.

She dragged in a deep breath, then another. The air was fresh. There was no stink of blood, feces, or rot.

"We did it." She sat up, ignoring her aches, and looked down at him.

That's when his hand fell away from her.

"Galen?" Her pulse spiked. His eye was closed. She pressed a palm to his chest and realized it wasn't moving. He wasn't breathing. "No. Galen!"

Sam scrambled up on her knees beside him. She'd been trained in advanced first aid and she quickly tilted his head back. She pressed her hands to his chest and pumped. Then she leaned over, closing her mouth over his, and breathed.

"Come on. Everyone says you're tough." She worked through the chest compressions, then breathed into him again. "Everyone talks about Imperator Galen in hushed voices. They are half afraid of you, or half in awe of you."

She kept up the pumps followed by the breaths.

"Breathe, damn you." Tears burned in her eyes as she looked at him. He was such an amazing specimen of man, and she knew he'd already suffered so much. He'd survived the destruction of his planet, and he hadn't just survived on Carthago, he'd thrived here. "Don't leave me alone, boss-man."

Suddenly, he heaved in a breath and his eye opened.

Sam slumped forward. "Thank God." She cupped his cheeks. "You are *not* dying on me."

"Not today." His voice sounded like gravel.

She pressed her forehead to his and just breathed. "You aren't allowed to scare me like that."

"Sam?"

She met his gaze.

"Thank you," he murmured.

She nodded and they stayed there while he recovered.

"We need shelter." He cupped the back of her head and curled up to sit. He looked around them, a muscle ticking in his jaw.

She followed his gaze. Sand, as far as the eye could see. Her gut curdled, her earlier elation evaporating away. They needed shelter and water, or they'd die out here. And all that effort to escape would have been for nothing.

"Come on." It took her a while, but she helped him to his feet. He was a little unsteady at first, but she watched his set face as he found his balance.

Almost dying couldn't stop Imperator Galen.

"Which direction?" she asked.

"East," he said.

They started moving through the sand. "No way I'm going to let a bit of sand beat me."

He glanced at her. "Carthago's deserts are deadly."

"Are you always this chipper?"

He frowned. "Chipper?"

"Focused on the doom and gloom."

"I'm a realist."

She snorted. "We are going to make it, Galen. And when we do, you'll owe me big time."

"Really?"

"Yep. I want shiny, expensive things. I've lived in a hellhole for months, with nothing but these rags. I want a new wardrobe, and a huge, soft bed—" she moaned a little "—with a super-soft blanket that feels like a cloud."

"You've put some thought into this."

Her smile faltered. "I needed to think of something to get me through."

His hand tightened on her hip and squeezed. "What else did you imagine?"

"Blooming flowers and food. Fresh fruit, like the sweetest berries, and chocolate, it's—"

"I know what it is. The human members of my house mention it...a lot."

27

She smiled. "I want homecooked meals. And I want to see art. A beautiful painting that reaches inside your chest and makes you feel. Anything except moldy rock walls."

"You're not what I expected, Sam Santos."

She smiled again. "I'm one-of-a-kind."

"Yes, I'm beginning to see that."

CHAPTER THREE

G alen had never met a more stubborn, determined woman.

He'd been wrong about Sam's essence being threaded with steel. It was made solely from the strongest, most impenetrable metal in the galaxy.

They'd been walking for hours. They were holding each other up, staggering through the sand. The suns were scorching hot in the sky above, and Galen's mouth was beyond dry. He knew if they didn't find water soon...

"Sam—"

"You tell me to leave you one more time and I'll hit you."

He grunted. So stubborn.

They started down the other side of a large dune and Galen prayed they'd stay on their feet. Beyond lay nothing but a sea of golden-orange sand.

"Tell me about the House of Galen," she asked.

"I run an orderly, profitable house. I have the best

gladiators in Kor Magna, and Raiden is the Champion of the Arena."

"And he and Harper are a couple?"

"Yes. Completely in love and devoted to each other. She's brilliant in the arena, and together, they are truly something to watch in a fight."

"I'm glad." Sam sighed. "Harper is a good woman."

"And my gladiator Thorin is with Regan Forrest."

"I didn't know her well. She worked hard on her experiments on the station and was shy." Sam shook her head. "Hard to imagine her with an alien gladiator."

"They make it work. Another gladiator, Kace, is married to Rory Fraser."

"Rory? The engineer from Fortuna Station?"

"Yes. They have a son."

"What?" Sam's voice was shocked. "It's been hard for me to keep track of time here, but how could they have a child already?"

"My healers tell me that Kace's genetics resulted in a far shorter gestation period than you have on Earth. They're both happy. Kace was former military, and Rory softened his hard edges."

Sam looked up at Galen, something working across her face. "Tell me more. Tell me about the other humans."

Galen told her more about his tough gladiator Saff and Blaine Strong, Lore and Madeline, as well as Mia, Dayna, Winter, Neve, Ever, and Ryan, and the men they'd attached themselves to.

"Madeline Cochran? My uptight former space-

"Sam."

"Shit." She moved in closer to him. "What is it?"

"No *drakking* idea."

A bunch of tentacles burst out of the sand. Several aimed straight at Sam, wrapping around her body and trapping her sword by her side. They tightened, coiling around her.

Galen strode forward, hacking at the tentacles he could reach. A deep, rumbling sound reverberated up from beneath the sand.

And then the tentacles moved, yanking Sam onto her back and dragging her along the sand.

Drak. Galen raced after her. Every time he got close to a tentacle, he slashed at it.

He lifted his sword to swing again—

But a tentacle wrapped around his bicep, holding his arm in place. Beneath them, the entire sand dune moved.

Drak.

The creature under the sand was huge. He'd heard rumors and legends of giant beasts deep in the heart of the desert before, but he'd never seen one like this.

Another tentacle wrapped around his knees. He was tackled into the sand as well, and then found himself being dragged alongside Sam. Galen muttered some savage curses. He arched his head and saw that somehow Sam had managed to get one of her arms free.

Galen swiveled onto his stomach and that's when he saw it—the giant, sucking mouth buried in the sand ahead.

They were being dragged straight toward it.

"*Ay Dios mío.*" Sam struggled. "No way."

They reached the mouth of the monster. The tentacles released him and Sam, giving each of them a final shove toward the yawning mouth.

Desperately, Galen reached out, grabbing the fleshy side of the mouth. It didn't have any teeth, and it was all soft and squishy. From down below, the stench of rotting meat rose up from the darkness. His gut curdled.

Sam flew past him, and with his other hand, Galen grabbed for her. He managed to snag her ankle.

"Galen." Her voice was short and sharp.

He gritted his teeth, taking her full weight. "I've...got you."

He paused for a second and took a deep breath, then he started to pull himself up. With Sam's additional weight, it was slow going, and it wasn't long before his already aching muscles were burning from the strain.

"Galen, I'm too heavy!"

"Won't let you go."

"Stubborn fool. You'll kill us both. Let me go and get out of here."

He wouldn't give up. He never gave up.

Galen pulled himself up over the edge of the creature's mouth, and then heaved Sam up after him.

She fell down on the sand, panting. "Damn, you're strong."

A deep rumble came from the giant's mouth beside them. Galen was well aware that even though they rested on sand, the monster was still below them, and no doubt had more tentacles.

Sam grabbed his hand. "How about we rest somewhere else?"

"Excellent idea."

Together, they jogged away from the monster, stumbling down the dune. Tentacles burst up out of the sand again and they dodged the fleshy limbs, swinging their swords.

Galen hacked off another tentacle and the creature screeched and retreated. Soon, they stumbled onto rockier ground.

"Think we're clear." Sam gasped for breath.

They made it to the top of the neighboring dune, and they both dropped to their knees. Behind them, they watched the mouth and tentacles sink back below the sand.

"I think we should keep going," Galen said.

"No complaints from me."

But even with their arms supportively around each other, their injuries and dehydration were taking a toll. Galen lost track of how long and far they'd traveled. He was soaked with sweat, and his body was a mass of agony.

Then Sam collapsed on the sand.

"Sam, no." He dropped down beside her, pulling at her arm.

She leaned into him, her eyes closed.

Drak. Fighting the creature had taken the last of their energy reserves. They were exhausted and thirsty. They couldn't go on.

Then Sam stared over his shoulder, eyes blinking. "Now I know I'm hallucinating."

He turned and saw several twisted rock formations in the distance. His chest tightened.

And beneath them was shade.

SAM STUMBLED in under a twist of rock that formed an arch. She had her shoulder wedged under Galen's arm, and at this point, she had no idea who was holding up whom.

As soon as she felt shade, she collapsed. Galen dropped down beside her.

She didn't care about the hard landing. They were in the shade. Blessed shade.

Sam closed her eyes. It was so good to be out of the sunlight. It was also definitely good not to be digesting in the belly of a giant sand beast.

As they dragged themselves up against the rock formations, she felt so thirsty she wanted to cry. In an attempt to distract herself, she studied the giant, protruding boulders around them. The rock here was fascinating—all different shades of gold, and twisted up like ribbons. One strand was a translucent gold that made her think of amber.

"I can smell water," Galen said.

Her throat spasmed and she groaned. "You must be dreaming. Please don't talk about water."

But she felt Galen pull himself up to a sitting position. When she leaned back against the rock, she froze. She felt a touch on her skin—something cool...and damp.

"Wait." She twisted around to stare at the rock. Galen moved closer and cursed softly.

The amber-like stone contained water.

Sam lifted her sword and gouged at the amber rock.

She watched the water pool in the impression she'd made.

"Ladies first," Galen said.

She cupped her hands and scooped the water out of the indentation in the rock. She drank fiercely. "I'm not feeling much like a lady right now." She drank more, moaning.

When she lifted her head, Galen's icy gaze was on her. Except he didn't look cold. She saw something hot on that rugged face, and she felt an answering tug inside her.

She cleared her throat. "Your turn."

He waited for water to pool, and then leaned forward to drink. When they'd both had enough, they leaned back against the rock, shoulder to shoulder.

Sam let her gaze wander over their surroundings. More rock formations were sprinkled randomly around them. It made her think of some art museum with statues on display. If she squinted, she imagined the formations made different shapes—a man riding a horse, a ship blasting into space, a couple locked in a passionate embrace.

Sleepiness washed over her. *Dios*, there wasn't a part of her that wasn't sore, and she felt a sharp pain in her belly that should probably concern her, but there wasn't much she could do. Her eyes fluttered closed and she felt herself doze. She hadn't slept well for months. At Zaabha, she couldn't risk falling into a deep sleep, not knowing what her captors, or some enterprising prisoner out to take on the Champion of Zaabha, might do to her.

When she woke, she found herself pressed against Galen's chest, his heart beating solidly under her ear. She blinked, her gaze on the tattoos inked on the skin of his arm.

"You're awake." Galen's low voice rumbled beneath her.

"Yes. Was I asleep long?"

She felt, rather than saw, the shake of Galen's head. "No."

Sam thought that perhaps she should get up, move away, maybe put some space between the two of them, but she found she didn't want to. She couldn't. Instead, she leaned into the warmth and strength that was Galen.

"Did you sleep?" she asked.

"No. I wanted to stay on guard."

Warmth twisted in her belly. "Thanks. Been a long time since someone watched over me."

Even as a child, she'd been taking charge and responsible. She was the oldest child and the big sister, and when she'd been sixteen, her father had suffered a stroke. Her mother had fallen apart and while her father had recovered, it had been Sam who'd held things together. Even back then, no one had watched over her, she'd watched over all of them.

Her gaze fell on Galen's tattoos. "Do these have meaning?" She touched her finger to his bicep, tracing the design. It was beautiful, depicting buildings that looked like they were out of some fantasy world.

"Every one of them has meaning. I got my first when I joined the academy to train as a royal guard."

"How old were you?"

"Eight."

She gasped. "So young."

"I knew I'd be assigned to the prince, who was just a toddler at the time." Galen sighed. "Seems so *drakking* long ago."

"The tattoos are beautiful."

"I usually cover them."

She sucked in a breath. "Why?"

"For Aurelians, inking your skin is a vow." He looked at his arm. "These signify my vow to protect Raiden and the Aurelian Royal family. To guard them with my life."

And clearly he felt like he'd failed. The raw guilt buried in his deep voice scraped over her. She understood. She'd been in charge of security at Fortuna and it had been destroyed.

But this wasn't about her, it was about him.

"What happened to your planet, Galen?"

"It's gone. All gone. The Thraxian mercenaries planted powerful bombs in the planet's fault lines. It was torn apart. I barely survived getting Raiden off the planet. We came here with nothing."

"Except your fighting skills." And survivor's guilt. How would it feel to be the only two people to survive your planet's destruction?

His lips moved. "Except those. And a whole lot of fury to burn off. When we came to Kor Magna, I went into the arena."

"And then you created the House of Galen and built a good life here."

"I survived."

Quiet fell between them.

"So what does the great Imperator Galen do for fun?" Sam asked.

He frowned. "Run my House."

She turned to look at him. "That's work."

"Train my gladiators. Rescue prisoners not suited to the arena."

She stared at him.

He cleared his throat. "Lately, I've been busy rescuing wayward humans."

"*Fun*, Galen, not work."

"My life is my House."

She shook her head. "I can't say I'm surprised. Alpha males just can't switch off. Fun means doing something you enjoy, things that relax you."

His brows drew together like the word *relax* was a foreign concept. "What do you do for fun?"

"I like to cook."

His eyebrows rose.

She grinned. "Just because I can fight doesn't mean I'm not rather talented in the kitchen. My mother taught all of us to cook, and I enjoy experimenting. When we get out of this desert, I'll cook for you." Pain stabbed in her belly and she wrapped an arm around herself.

"I'll hold you to that." Galen frowned, eyeing the way she was cradling her body. "You're in pain."

"Those tentacles squeezed me hard, and I'm pretty sure I'd already bruised a few ribs in the fall." She winced. "It'll be fine."

"Let me see."

As his hands touched her leather corset, she tried to push him away. "No—"

He ignored her, pushing the tattered leather up. He hissed.

She looked down, knowing what she'd see. Terrible bruising mottled her skin.

"Sam," he breathed.

"There's nothing we can do."

His gaze met hers. "You have internal bleeding."

"I know, but like I said, there's nothing we can do out here."

His face hardened. "We need to get you medical help."

She swallowed. "I won't be able to go that far."

"I'll carry you."

"You could barely walk earlier, Galen."

But he rose, and a second later, he scooped her off the ground like she weighed no more than a sword. She started to struggle, but he made a sound and she stopped.

Then he started walking.

"Galen."

"Quiet."

She shook her head, sliding her arm along his broad shoulders. "And you said I was stubborn."

He pushed onward through the forest of rock formations, but their progress was slow. The suns were both still high in the sky, and even though he stuck to the shade where he could, the heat remained unbearable.

So was the growing pain.

It wasn't long before Sam felt her consciousness start slipping away. "I'm not going to make it." It seemed unfair to finally escape Zaabha, only to have the desert and her injuries kill her.

"You will."

He spoke forcefully, his tone like iron. She wanted to believe him.

"I would've liked to see the House of Galen."

"You will, Sam."

"I would've liked to cook for you."

"You *will*. I like this certain vegetable the chef gets from the market. It's called *fidea*. I've never told him that it's my favorite. I'll have him get an entire crate of it, and you can show me what you can do."

Her head lolled against his shoulder. "Hmm."

"Hold on, Sam."

She stared at the lines of strain bracketing his mouth. He was in pain too, but she knew he'd die trying to save her. He stumbled several times, but his steps never faltered.

He was a man who would never give up.

"Stubborn man." Unable to hold her head up anymore, she turned her face against his neck.

Sam had no idea how long they'd traveled, because she felt herself drifting in and out of consciousness. The next thing she knew, Galen went down heavily on one knee, still clutching her to his chest.

Ahead, she saw that the suns had almost set, and shadows were chasing across the desert. In among the rock formations, she watched the shadows shift and dance.

She blinked. Wait a second?

"Galen?"

He pulled her closer, and then she heard him curse.

They appeared out of nowhere. With dark, haughty faces and weapons clutched in their hands. One glance, and she knew these people were warriors. They were tall, lean, and muscled, with dark, patterned skin. The pattern matched the rock around them. Long, dreadlocked hair fell past their shoulders.

"Desert wraiths," Galen murmured quietly. "They can change their skin color and pattern to camouflage themselves."

Sam's muscles tensed. She'd heard of them. In the dark corners of Zaabha, she'd heard people whisper of the deadly killers of the desert. She'd even seen a few in the arena.

She tried to pull herself up, but pain speared through her. She tried to stay with Galen, but finally the darkness sucked her down into a dark hole, and as she fell, she knew there was no way she could climb back out.

CHAPTER FOUR

G alen jerked awake. He was floating in something
warm.

He lifted his head, and discovered that he was lying
in a warm, mineral pool. The sharp smell of the mineral-
enhanced water filled his nostrils.

He sat up slowly and gingerly, and noted he was free
of pain. Then he realized a couple of things. One, he was
resting on a flat, shallow rock that sat just below the
water, and two, he was naked.

He looked around and saw he was in a cave. He
noted the single tunnel leading into the space. Beside
him, he saw Sam resting in the pool, with the water
lapping at her body. Her naked body.

Galen's teeth snapped together. The water didn't
quite cover her breasts, leaving her dark pink nipples
bare. Her hair spread around her, floating in the water.

Something inside him went still as his gaze moved
over her. She was gorgeous. He liked the enticing mix of

muscle, strength, and curves. It had been a very long time since a woman had tempted him this much. Her chest rose and fell with each breath, and her bruises had faded to almost nothing. Her skin glowed a beautiful golden-brown in the dim, lantern light that lit the cave.

He forced himself to drag his gaze off her. Instead, he moved his arms and legs. It was a relief to not feel any pain. Looking down at the cloudy water, he realized that it must have some sort of healing properties.

Suddenly, he heard a faint splash and saw Sam sitting up, blinking. She pushed her wet hair off her face.

"*Dios mío.*" She turned her head and then blinked at him.

Galen was used to nakedness. Gladiators trained together, showered together, patched up their injuries together. "Sam? You okay?"

Her gaze drifted down his body, over his chest and abs, then snagged on his cock. A cock that had surged to life when he'd first seen her. She blinked again, and Galen felt a spurt of pleasure at the heat in her gaze.

Then she shook her head, like she was trying to clear it. "Ah, I think so. You're really naked."

He fought back a smile and stood. "So are you."

He heard her make a strangled sound as he left the pool. He thankfully found a stack of drying cloths at the water's edge. Nabbing one, he wrapped it around his hips. "How do you feel?"

Sam slithered off the stone and sank into the water in a deeper part of the pool. "*Bueno.* I feel...amazing."

"These are healing pools."

"You're better?" she asked.

He nodded. "There's no pain."

"I'm assuming the desert wraiths didn't kill us."

"I lost consciousness just after you did. But unless this is the afterlife, I'm guessing we're in wraith territory."

Her gaze moved over his chest again. "I haven't felt this good in ages. Like I'm buzzing with energy."

Galen snatched up another drying cloth and held it out for her. He forced himself to stare at the rock wall as she climbed out. He heard the water splash, the slap of her wet footsteps, and his brain became obsessed with imagining the water running down her body, clinging to that golden skin.

She wrapped the cloth around her, and when he deemed it safe to look back, he learned to his dismay that the damp fabric stuck to her, turning transparent.

His cock hardened more and he swallowed a groan. He couldn't remember the last woman he'd taken to his bed. When he'd first arrived on Carthago and fought in the arena, he'd had his fill of meaningless, easy sex. There was always someone keen to share a gladiator's bed. Later, he'd lost interest in the women who were out to cross an imperator off their scorecard.

But in truth, he'd only ever allowed himself quick, empty couplings. He'd had a job to do—providing for Raiden, winning fights, and building his House. Wallowing in pleasure hadn't been a part of his plan.

Sam raised her arms, lifting her wet hair off her shoulders. Her breasts were perfectly outlined, full and tempting, and her nipples were hard.

He looked away. She'd just escaped a nightmare and

needed time to heal. What she didn't need was someone taking advantage of her.

"Galen." Her voice was low and husky. She reached out and touched his shoulder.

He looked down into her face.

"Thank you," she murmured. "For getting me out."

He shook his head. "Sam, you got me out."

"We did it together. We're not a bad team." She stepped closer.

His muscles went taut. "Sam—"

"Galen." A smile moved her lips.

"You just survived hell." He could hardly miss the thick tension pumping between them. And she could hardly miss his cock tenting the drying cloth. "You need time to heal."

"I'm feeling healthy." She moved her shoulders which drew his gaze.

He saw a drop of water run down her neck, then down her collarbone. He wanted to lick it up with his tongue. He ground his teeth together. He was used to controlling his wants and needs.

"I don't feel any pain, and I'm pretty fucking happy to be alive." She took another step, her breasts brushing against his chest. "I like what I see when I look at you."

Drak. Galen's hands curled into fists, he didn't move.

"I want to kiss you," she said.

His gaze moved to hers. To those brown eyes that looked like deep pools.

She smiled. "Just a kiss."

"It's not a good idea."

"Why?"

"Because."

Her eyebrows rose. "That's all you've got? Because?"

He gripped her arms. "*Drak*, Sam. I'm trying to take care of you."

She moved up on her toes. "Then say yes."

Something inside him snapped. He yanked her closer.

He crashed his mouth down on hers, sliding his hands into her wet hair. Hunger shot through him, and he parted her lips with his tongue, sliding inside. She moaned, and the sound vibrated through him.

Sam's hands gripped his shoulders, her fingers digging into his skin. He drank deep and her tongue slid against his, demanding more. This was no sweet, submissive woman who'd let him lead. She'd take, demand, and give back.

Galen felt strength pour through him. A woman who matched him, step for step. He felt alive, his body pulsing with desire. She tasted even better than he'd imagined, and he found her strength intoxicating.

When they finally broke apart, she looked dazed. "Jesus."

He dragged in a breath, trying to find his equilibrium. *Drak*, she'd scrambled his brain. Then he heard a faint sound.

Spinning, he pulled her close, and faced the tunnel leading into the cave. "Someone's coming."

Several desert wraiths appeared at the cave entrance. Galen tried to push Sam back behind him, but she elbowed him and moved right up beside him.

His mouth flattened into a line, and he shook his head

wryly. He should be used to Earth women ignoring his orders by now.

"Imperator Galen," the wraith in the lead murmured.

The man was more muscular than most of his brethren. His chest was bare and streaked with white pigment, and he wore trousers made of the hide of some desert beast. He had a proud face, his dark, dreadlocked hair almost reaching to his waist. Twin curved swords hung at his hips.

Galen bowed his head. "Thank you for helping us."

The man watched him. "My name is Catto. I know you assisted Zisa and her clan to the east of here."

Zisa had lost clan members to a crazy genius who'd holed up in the desert and had also purchased Mia for his high-tech experiments. Galen had led his team in to free her and the man's other captives. "It was my pleasure to help bring down Catalyst and free Zisa's people."

Catto tilted his head. "And now you have another mission."

Galen felt Sam shift closer to him, their arms brushing.

"You know of Zaabha?" Sam asked.

"The floating devil city." There were hushed, angry murmurs from the other wraiths in the room.

"There are people trapped there, forced to fight to the death," Sam said.

The wraith leader glanced at her. "We will give you assistance to regain your strength and return to your House."

Sam took a step forward. "I can see you're warriors. You could help us bring it down—"

Galen wrapped his hand around her arm and pulled her back. His gaze met the wraith's. "We are grateful for your help."

Catto inclined his head. "Rest. We will bring you food and clothes."

"We need to get back to Kor Magna," Galen said.

The wraith nodded again. "At nightfall, my warriors will escort you to the Al-Maa Trading Post."

And leave them there to find their own way home. It was more than Galen expected. He was grateful they'd saved their lives.

The wraiths turned to leave, melding into the shadows around them.

"They won't fight?" Sam asked.

"It's not their way."

"I saw some of their people at Zaabha, Galen. Most of them refused to fight and were killed by the Thraxians."

"And we will rescue any who remain prisoner. For now, we rest, and then we get back to the House of Galen."

She nodded. "And then?"

"Then we put together our army to stop the Thraxians and destroy Zaabha."

SAM WOKE SNUGGLED in Galen's arms, her cheek pressed to a firm chest.

Dios, he was so hard. She breathed him in. He smelled like dark spice and male. Parts of her that had been dead for so long flared to life. Desire made her dizzy, and she felt the throb between her legs.

She barely knew him, and yet, she felt like they were connected. After everything they'd been through, they weren't strangers.

It was just the intense situation making her feel like this. They'd fought side by side, escaped Zaabha and the desert monster. That connected people.

She looked up at his face and the glossy black patch over his eye. Sleep did nothing to soften him. He looked like a slumbering warlord—always ready for battle, even when he was resting. Any second, he'd leap up, sword in hand.

She blew out a breath. She was attracted to him. This wasn't just some delusion of adrenaline combined with their dangerous situation.

Sam, you don't need the complication of a man. Life had been hard these last few months. She needed to get her feet back under her, to be steady for a while, before she thought of anything else.

What if she ended up back in Zaabha? Her muscles locked. What if the Thraxians came for her? Her innermost fears bubbled up, clogging her throat.

She rolled away from Galen, but an arm snaked around her waist. It tightened and pulled her back.

"Where are you going?" His deep voice was low and husky.

She looked around the cave. There was nowhere to go. "Well—"

"Relax." He pulled her back to his chest. "We have a bit longer until the suns set."

She frowned. They were underground. "How do you know?"

"I can sense it."

She settled back against him. It was easy to forget that he was an alien. He certainly looked human. "What other abilities does your species have?"

"I can sense essences. Essentially what a person's personality is like."

"Handy."

"And Aurelians are bred tough. We're stronger and hardier than we look."

"How come most species I've seen look humanoid?"

"Because of the Creators."

"Creators?"

"An ancient, advanced species who created life in the galaxy. They seeded life on habitable planets, and created sentient beings in their own likeness."

"Wow. What happened to them?"

"No one knows. They disappeared millennia ago, leaving the species they created and some ruins behind."

As they lay there, she felt his hand stroking her hair. Again, she felt a curl of heat low in her belly.

"Feeling better?" he asked.

Except for wanting to jump your bones. She nodded and moved her head. Her lips accidentally brushed against his skin. She felt him tense beneath her.

Sam had always been upfront about sex. If she saw a guy she liked, she asked him out. It hadn't happened a lot. Work, especially working on a space station, had kept her pretty busy. She never dated people she worked with, so her hookups were limited to her trips back to Earth.

Her last relationship had been a disaster. Rex had been a high-powered businessman in New San Francisco. On their last date, she'd saved him from being mugged. Instead of the thank you she'd expected, he'd been angry. Told her everything she did emasculated him and that she wasn't feminine enough. She'd dumped the asshole as quick as she could.

Unfortunately, most of the men before Rex hadn't been much better.

She breathed Galen in. She was pretty sure that nothing she did would make Galen feel emasculated. She tried to remind herself that Galen was a man holding the fate of all the surviving humans in his scarred palm.

But her body wasn't listening. She moved her hand, rubbing her fingers over his flat nipple.

He groaned and they both went still.

"Galen." She looked up at his face and she saw something working in his crystal-blue eye.

"Sam...you're vulnerable..."

She smiled at his obvious line of thought. "And you're not going to take advantage of me, right?"

"Correct."

She moved her fingers over his chest, caressing the hard slabs of muscle. "What if I want you to take advantage of me?"

He sucked in a breath and reared up. He pushed her onto her back and rolled on top of her. "No."

Sam felt the rapid beat of his heart under her palms and an ugly thought slid into her head. "You don't want me?" Maybe Galen liked sweet, pretty little things that made him feel big and strong.

His hand gripped her wrist. "We both know that isn't true," he growled.

Her tense muscles relaxed and she slid a hand up to cup his stubbled cheek.

"But you've been through an ordeal," he added.

"Galen?"

His eye glittered. "What?"

"Shut up." She pushed, rolling until he was flat on his back, and she straddled him. She leaned down and kissed him.

His hands clamped on her hips, his tongue thrusting into her mouth. Oh, so good. The kiss was hard and rough, and she wanted it to never end. Liquid heat poured through her, and her only thought was that nothing had ever felt so good, so right.

The kiss deepened, turning fierce. Galen rolled them again until he was on top, his body fully settling on hers. She loved the solid weight of him, and the hard bulge of his cock between her legs. A very generous cock. She lifted her hips, grinding against him. A groan tore through him, mingling with her own husky cries.

"I'm sorry to interrupt." The low voice of the wraith leader.

Galen froze then pressed his forehead to hers.

"Night is falling," Catto said. "We've brought you some food and clothes."

Galen gathered himself, pushed off Sam, and rose. "Thank you. For all your assistance."

The wraith nodded and left.

Sam sat up. The drying cloth did nothing to hide Galen's large, erect cock. She swallowed.

He grabbed one of the plates the wraiths had left. "Here." He set the food down for her.

She didn't recognize a single thing, but her mouth watered. Everything looked fresh and wonderfully edible. There was nothing that stank or was rotting. She started trying things—sweet fruits, tasty meats, something she thought might be a kind of cheese.

Galen popped a few things in his mouth, then moved to the pile of clothes resting on a rock. Sam didn't even pretend not to watch as he dressed. He pulled on black leather trousers, giving her a brief flash of a muscular flank, and then fastened a leather harness across his chest.

After her belly was full, she fished around in the clothes and pulled on a pair of leather trousers of her own. They were slightly too small, which made her think they'd originally been made for a child, and cupped her ass like an eager lover, but they were better than anything she'd been given at Zaabha. She pulled on a beige shirt that felt soft on her skin, and tucked it into her trousers. Galen's boots and her sandals had been cleaned and returned. Lastly, she strapped her sword on.

She turned and found Galen watching her.

"Ready to go?" he asked.

She nodded. He looked at her with a flat stare, like they hadn't kissed or touched each other. She sighed. Maybe it was better this way. Better not to succumb to this crazy, intense desire that would complicate everything for them.

They headed out of the cave, and two wraith guards met them. Silently, they followed the wraiths through the twisting tunnels and came out into the night-drenched desert.

Ahead, she saw the wraith leader standing beside a large, cat-like beast. Sam sucked in a breath. She'd seen similar creatures in the arena—they liked to tear their prey apart.

But this one sat quietly, watching them with calm, golden eyes. It reminded her of a black panther, just bigger. It also had a blanket tied onto its back.

Catto waved at the beast and Galen strode forward. He climbed on, finding his seat. Sam climbed on behind him, wrapping her arms around his hard body.

"It is a short run to the trading post," the wraith leader said. "We will escort you to the gates."

Someone let out a sharp whistle, and the beast sprang into action. Sam gripped Galen harder, watching as he directed the beast with the simple leather reins. Several wraiths fell into step beside them, running alongside with ease. They were fast and nearly invisible. *Amazing.*

She had no idea how far the trading post was, but the minutes turned to hours. Carthago's moons rose up into the sky, brighter than the moon on Earth. For the first time, she let herself enjoy the view. She'd only ever seen them from Zaabha's arena, but now, wrapped around Galen's warm body, feeling fed and clean, she watched the moons and felt something inside her relax. She had to admit that even though much of Carthago could kill, the planet possessed a harsh beauty she liked.

Some of the wraiths were murmuring in their quiet language, and the sound caught her ear.

"Look," Galen said.

Peering over Galen's shoulder, Sam spotted the glow of light on the horizon.

As they got closer, she saw a large, metal fence surrounding a desert village. The Al-Maa Trading Post. Galen pulled the beast to a halt some distance from the gates. They were close enough now that from inside, she heard raucous laughter.

"This is where we leave you," the wraith leader said. "Travel well, Imperator Galen."

"Thank you again." Galen bowed his head.

In a blink, the wraiths were gone. Sam strained to see them, but it was like they were never there. The beast they'd ridden bounded into the darkness after them.

Galen grabbed her hand and pulled her towards the trading post entrance.

A bored-looking guard sitting above the gate eyed them for a moment before he lifted a hand and flicked a finger. One of the large gates creaked open just enough to let them inside. As they entered, Sam's gaze landed on deep, jagged scratches in the metal.

"What the hell did that?" she asked.

"Night beasts. The desert is filled with some unfriendly creatures, especially after the suns have set."

Sam was happy when the door clanged shut behind them.

Inside, the place looked as though she'd stepped back in time. The buildings were made of beige, clay-like bricks with dome-shaped roofs. The trading post was laid out haphazardly around a few dusty streets, and she saw several large pens filled with numerous kinds of beasts that she assumed people rode and traded.

She glanced at Galen. He was eyeing the place impassively. "What now?"

"We need to contact the House of Galen." He strode forward, pulling her with him.

As they headed down the street, passing some open-fronted stalls selling goods and food, she could hardly believe she was out of Zaabha. Here, people were going about their daily lives, most likely completely unaware of the horror that floated in the sky somewhere above them, and it felt a bit surreal to her.

Galen stopped in front of the building that Sam guessed had to be a bar. A bright light blinked above the entrance, and inside, she heard the rumble of conversation punctuated by wild laughs and music. She might be half a galaxy away from Earth, but some things were the same.

Inside, the building was filled with a haze of smoke. People huddled around small tables, or sat at the long bar at the back. On one side of the space was a small stage, where a thin, green-skinned woman with dreadlocks writhed desultorily.

Galen nodded to the bar. As they reached it, a large, alien bartender looked up from cleaning dirty glasses with a rag. Sam hadn't seen his species before. He had brown skin, hulking shoulders, and a single eye resting in the center of his forehead.

"I need a communicator," Galen said.

The bartender's set face didn't change. "Tech don't work well out here."

"I'll pay."

The bartender ran his gaze over their simple clothes and lack of gear. "Don't think you can."

"I'll pay when my people arrive," Galen amended.

The bartender shook his head. "Only take upfront payment."

Galen pressed his palms to the bar and leaned forward. "Listen—"

Sam drew her sword, and in a flash, held the tip against the bartender's throat. "You're speaking with an imperator, so show some respect."

The man's eye widened, and his gaze moved to Galen's face and eyepatch. "Galen," he breathed.

Galen shot her an amused look, before he turned back to the bartender and inclined his head.

"There is no charge for the Imperator of the House of Galen." The big man threw his rag on the bar. "This way."

CHAPTER FIVE

"I f the night beasts get you, don't say I didn't warn you."

Galen ignored the guard's warning and strode out of the gates of the trading post. Sam followed right behind him. Stars dotted the night sky above, but in the distance, one light was brighter than the others.

It wasn't a star, it was the light of an approaching ship.

They waited in silence, but Galen continuously scanned their surroundings. He was getting Sam out of there safely and wasn't going to let a hungry night beast take a bite out of them.

The ship roared overhead, lights illuminating the ground and engines kicking up sand as it landed.

"Holy hell." Sam looked up, her gaze glued to the sleek ship.

Galen watched as the ramp at the side of the ship lowered, and his gladiators strode out.

Sam stared, taking them all in. "They sure know how to make an entrance."

Raiden's red cloak whipped around behind him. He had a sword held in his hand and Harper was by his side. Behind them came the rest of his gladiators, all carrying swords, axes, and staffs.

As Raiden neared, a smile lit up his face. "Should have known you wouldn't wait for us to rescue you."

"You were taking too long." He and Raiden slapped each other on the back.

Saff pushed forward and gave Galen a tight hug. "*Don't* do that again."

He turned his head and saw that Sam was flanked by Harper and Blaine. They were smiling and hugging each other.

It was time to go home.

"We've had a hell of a few days." Galen took Sam's arm. "Let's get Sam off her feet."

He led her up the ramp and into the shuttle. The ship's interior was decorated in shades of gray, and everything was slick and streamlined. Rows of comfortable seats filled the back of the shuttle, and the front narrowed to the high-tech cockpit.

Galen's gaze fell on the man in the pilot's chair. Rillian—owner of the Dark Nebula Casino—was, as always, polished and immaculate. Beside him, in the co-pilot's chair, was his woman, Dayna. The human woman jumped to her feet and rushed over to give Sam a hug.

"It is so good to see you," Dayna said.

"You too." Sam glanced at Rillian, and then around the ship. "Thanks for the ride."

"Our pleasure." Rillian smiled as he tapped the console in front of him. "Now, everyone strap in. We need to get moving. This journey is testing the limits of the ship's desert capabilities."

Dayna quickly explained to Sam about minerals in the sand that messed up engines and technology. She led Sam over to one of the plush passenger chairs.

"*Drakking* good to see you alive, G," Raiden said.

"Good to be alive." Galen dragged in a breath. "It was touch and go, but we made it. Had some help from the local wraiths."

He saw his gladiators strapping in and moved to sit in the space beside Sam. They hadn't even left the trading post yet, and he found that he missed having her right beside him.

He pulled his belt on, and a second later, the ship rose straight up. Galen glanced out the long side window and watched the lights of Al-Maa disappear from view.

"Now, tell us what happened." Raiden demanded.

Galen looked at Sam. Together, they recounted the story of their escape from Zaabha.

"Implants?" Raiden eyed the remains of Sam's implant.

"The Thraxians are planning something," Sam said. "And it involves the implants."

"We just don't have all the details yet," Galen said.

"Sand suckers," Thorin growled.

Saff crossed her arms. "Crudspawn."

"Whatever they have planned, we will stop them," Galen said.

"You have a plan?" Kace asked.

"I'll need Zhim and Ryan to find everything they can on the implants. We need to reexamine Neve's implant, plus get whatever we can off Sam's, once it is removed." He saw her fingering the remains still attached to the side of her head.

"There is one main Thraxian scientist in charge of the implant research," Sam said. "He keeps everything on a data crystal in his lab at Zaabha."

Galen nodded. "Then we'll go in, destroy the data crystal, and capture the scientist. Then we free the prisoners and annihilate Zaabha once and for all."

"And the Thraxians, the Srinar, and the rest of their allies?" Raiden asked, something hard in his gaze.

"They will suffer their own fate," Galen said. "Imprisoned somewhere for the rest of their lives."

"Coming up on Kor Magna," Rillian called from the cockpit.

Galen unbuckled his belt, stood, and grabbed Sam's hand. As he led her over to a larger window, he was conscious of everyone watching them. He pulled her to the glass. "Welcome to Kor Magna."

"Wow," she murmured. "It looks like a carpet full of glowing jewels."

The lights of the city did look pretty against the darkness. "It's not so pretty in the daytime, but it has a lot to offer. You have a home here."

She looked up at him and smiled. "Thank you, Galen."

"Thank you, Sam. I would have died at Zaabha without your help."

"I'm not sure I believe that." Her face turned serious.

"I want in on the mission to end the Thraxians and Zaabha."

Everything inside Galen instantly rebelled. He was a protector by nature, born and bred. She'd just escaped that sand-sucking hellhole, and he didn't want her going anywhere near it again.

He didn't want to risk her, especially after everything she'd been through.

But her dark gaze steadily held his. There might be fear hidden in there, but it was buried beneath steely determination. He knew she was a warrior, a fighter, a gladiator.

There was also another part of him rising up, one that he had little experience with. A part that wanted to see Sam happy and give her whatever she wanted. Whatever she needed.

"As you wish."

SAM FINALLY FLICKED off the hot water in the shower. She'd been in there for close to an hour, and it had felt heavenly.

Naked, she stepped out onto the cool tiles of the bathroom connected to her new bedroom.

She wrapped herself in a large, soft, drying cloth. Her new room in the House of Galen, in the Kor Magna Arena, in the city of Kor Magna, on the alien planet of Carthago. She shook her head. Her life had sure taken a few unbelievable twists.

She released a breath and looked at herself in the

foggy mirror. She was trying to focus on her gorgeous, comfortable surroundings, but dark memories of her cell kept butting in. Even as she tried to take in the simple beauty of the room around her, she remembered cold rock, the scent of rotting food, the feel of arena sand beneath her feet, and the screams echoing in the air.

She sucked in another breath.

Maybe because none of this was really hers. She'd had nothing at Zaabha, and despite this luxurious suite around her, she still had nothing. Her wet hair dangled around her face, and she brushed it back, studying the metallic remnants of the implant stuck to her skin. She was getting the damn thing removed today, so maybe that would help her feel more normal.

The other human women were here at the House of Galen and in the city. They'd all survived, and Sam knew she would too. She'd make sure of it.

She moved out into the lovely bedroom. Gauzy, white curtains billowed over the arched windows looking out into the training arena below, and the room was dominated by the large bed she'd slept in the night before.

After only a few steps, she froze. Someone had been in her room while she'd showered.

The bed now had several soft-looking pillows stacked against the headboard, and a fluffy, gray blanket rested at the foot. Her chest tight, she moved over and stroked the fabric. It was exquisitely soft. Almost like a cloud.

On the bedside table was a large vase of alien flowers in a multitude of colors. A picture had been added to the wall. It was a painting of two full moons hanging in a beautiful night sky. It reminded her of riding on the beast in the desert with Galen.

Galen.

Sam pressed a closed fist to her heart. She stared at the things, the pretty things that she'd dreamed about, and dragged in some deep breaths.

Suddenly, the bedroom door slammed open and her fellow humans charged in.

"Time for breakfast," the red-headed Rory called out.

Something touched Sam's ankle and she looked down. A robot dog was sniffing at her feet.

"Don't mind Hero," Rory said. "He's just memorizing your scent."

"Where's your baby?" Sam asked.

"Having some daddy time. My gladiator is gaga for that kid."

"I have some clothes for you, courtesy of our generous imperator." Madeline bustled forward with an armload of various-colored fabrics. "Get dressed while we get breakfast set up on the balcony."

Sam just blinked at them. It had been so long since she'd spent time with friends. So long since anyone had cared. "Thank you."

In the bathroom, she pulled on a supple pair of leather pants and a deep-red shirt. Before she knew it, she was stepping out onto her balcony.

Sweet, blonde-haired Regan and Harper were supervising the workers setting food on the low tables. The rest of the women, including the small, blonde Mia, were sitting on large, comfy cushions. The tables were laden with all kinds of food—most that she didn't recognize, but that didn't matter. It smelled good.

Then, Sam heard the sound of swords clashing. Her gaze went past the railing and on the sand below, she saw a group of gladiator recruits training. There was a flash of red, and she spotted Raiden, with the large Thorin by his side. Her gaze sharpened as she took in some of the training moves.

"I thought you'd be sick of fighting," Regan said quietly.

Rory snorted. "I think she's taking in the view." The woman winked. "Can't complain about the view around here."

Sam picked up a green berry off a plate. "I'm more interested in seeing what the training involves."

Harper smiled. "Once a security officer, always a security officer."

Rory shoved a bread roll in her mouth. "Sure."

"Are you okay?" Harper's face was serious as she looked at Sam.

"To tell you the truth... No," Sam answered honestly. "Everything feels surreal. I keep thinking that at any moment, someone is going to grab me and drag me off to a cell."

The women fell silent, sympathy on their faces.

"We all understand, Sam," Regan said. "I used to have nightmares when I first arrived at the House of Galen."

"And none of us will ever forget the cells and captivity," Harper added.

Sam stiffened her spine. She knew they'd all been

through their own terrible ordeals with the Thraxians. "I keep waiting to wake up and find my escape was just a dream." She managed to smile at Harper. "But I will be okay."

Harper nodded. "It takes time. But just remember that you're safe and free."

"I had nightmares for a while too," Mia said.

"Mine finally stopped." Regan blushed prettily. "Especially when I'm snuggled up to my gladiator."

Sam tried to imagine the huge, wild Thorin snuggling and failed. "I'm so glad you're all okay." She let her gaze rest on each of the women. They all looked happy and healthy. "You are all okay, right? No one is forcing you—"

Laughter broke out around the table.

Regan leaned forward. "We are all in love with protective, alpha-male, alien gladiators."

"Galen took us in," Madeline said. "He moved mountains to help rescue all of us."

Regan nodded, her blonde hair shifting around her face. "He didn't just rescue us, he gave us all whatever we needed to heal. Like my lab."

"My job in maintenance," Rory added.

"I'm in the arena," Harper said. "Winter's working in Medical, that's why she isn't here this morning. Madeline's doing House administration, Mia's performing at the Dark Nebula Casino, and even though Galen wasn't happy about it, he let Dayna, Neve, Ever, and Ryan go with their men."

"He's a good guy," Madeline said. "He never asks for anything in return."

Sam felt all the women watching her expectantly.

She cleared her throat. "I know. He's a good fighter too. I would never have made it out without him."

"I saw the way he was with you on the ship," Harper said.

Sam reached out, grabbing a glass of some blue-tinted juice. "Galen watches everything, and he's protective to the bone."

"Yes, but he *watches* you," Harper said.

Rory leaned forward. "Really?" There was a gleeful tone to her voice.

Sam sipped the drink. It was good. "I know all of you are in love and happy, and you want to spread the joy..."

Rory pouted. "So nothing happened between the two of you?"

"We fought a ton of Thraxians and their fighters, jumped off a floating desert arena, almost got eaten by a huge desert beast that tried to drag us underground, and barely survived the desert. That's what happened between the two of us."

The women all stared at her with open mouths.

Harper patted her arm. "I am so glad you made it."

"Bummer," Rory said. "God, I so want to know how that man kisses." The redhead's gaze turned distant. "He's so controlled and in charge. I wonder what it's like when he lets loose."

Sam's gaze narrowed. "Don't you have a man?"

"Yes, but I'm still allowed to wonder what would make the oh-so-controlled Galen lose his control." Rory grinned. "Don't you wonder about kissing him?"

Sam looked away to the side and took another sip of her drink.

"Oh, my God," Regan breathed. "You've already kissed him."

The women all gasped.

"I'm not discussing this with you," Sam said.

"Why not?" Rory asked.

Harper crossed her arms. "All right, ladies. Leave her alone."

There was a knock on the bedroom door, and through the archway, Sam saw Galen enter her room.

The women all went silent, their eyes bugging out of their head. As one, they stared at him.

Sam did too. She figured that this was his standard uniform. Black leather trousers, a tight, black shirt that molded over his hard muscles, and a black cloak that fell back behind him. He looked hard and fierce and in control.

All the things that tripped Sam's trigger. *Big time.*

The women were looking at Galen, but when Sam sat back in her seat, she realized that Regan was watching her. Then the woman's gaze moved between her and Galen, and she giggled.

"Hey, G," Rory called out with a smile.

Galen took them all in, his face impassive. "Good morning." His icy-blue gaze zeroed in on Sam. "Sam, you're due at Medical."

For her implant removal. She stood and nodded at the women. "I'll see you all later. Thanks for breakfast."

As she left, she was followed by a wave of good-natured laughing and goodbyes.

She stepped into the hall with Galen. "Thank you."

"For what?" he asked.

"Well, again for rescuing me, but also for the lovely things you put in my room."

He looked ahead. "You're welcome." He was quiet for a minute, holding the door open for her. "You've been alone a long time, Sam, but you aren't alone anymore."

The warmth of his words carried her through the stone-lined corridors. She took in the House of Galen as they walked. It was clean, organized, and looked well-run. She'd expected nothing less. She glanced at one of the wall hangings on the wall, depicting gladiators in battle. It was a fine piece of art.

"I was hoping I could ask you something?" she said.

"Anything."

"I'd like to speak with my family."

He nodded. "I'll contact Zhim and organize it."

"Thanks." He just kept giving her things. She wished she could give something back.

He led her through a set of doors and she took in the neat, tidy Medical area of the House of Galen. She spied Winter, who was working with some of the tall Hermia healers. The human woman bustled up to her with a smile.

"Hi, Sam. So wonderful to see you."

That's when Sam noticed several tall men standing behind Winter. Men with metal arms and several metallic implants. Sam instantly stiffened. *Cyborgs*. After having her own implant forced on her and seeing the implanted fighters at Zaabha, the cyborgs left her wary.

Another woman pushed past the largest of the cyborgs. It was Ever Haynes, a woman Sam had helped at Zaabha. The woman was cradling a baby.

"Hi," Ever said. "I'm so glad you're safe, Sam."

"Ever." Sam's gaze fell on the baby. "I thought Rory had a baby."

"She does. So do I." Ever tilted the pink-wrapped bundle up to show a tiny, sleeping face with a cupid's-bow mouth. "This is Asha. Crazy, isn't it?"

Sam sucked in a breath. "You were pregnant at Zaabha?"

"Yes, and now I'm a mom." Ever shook her head, her dark hair sliding over her shoulder. "It's a crazy, complicated story, but my cyborg here is Asha's daddy." Ever nudged the big, silent Magnus Rone standing behind her.

Sam blinked. Somehow, Ever had given birth to the Imperator of the House of Rone's baby. She shook her head.

"Asha's name means hope, life." Ever smiled at her baby. "Seemed appropriate."

A hand touched Sam's shoulder and she felt the electric zing of Galen's touch.

"The House of Rone healers have more experience with implants and how they integrate with organic cells," Galen explained. "I asked Magnus if they could assist my healers in removing your implant."

Ever gripped Sam's arm. "There's nothing to it. They removed mine with no problems. This is Avarn." She nodded to a nearby older man, who had long, white hair pulled back in a ponytail. "He's head healer for the House of Rone."

The man inclined his head.

Sam set her shoulders back. "Right. Let's get this done, shall we?"

Following instructions, she climbed onto a bunk and lay down. She focused on the Hermia healer touching her head. The healer was tall and very slender, with a bald head and large green eyes. She knew they were genderless.

Someone shifted some equipment and a bright light shone in Sam's face. Her breath quickened and her pulse jumped. She'd spent some unpleasant time in the lab at Zaabha.

Flashbacks gripped her. Thraxian scientists poking and prodding, pain and screams.

"Sam?" Winter's concerned voice.

Sam swallowed, trying to fight her way through the flashbacks.

Firm fingers gripped her shoulder and squeezed. She scented Galen and instantly, the memories faded.

"I'm here," he said. "You're okay."

"They..." She swallowed. "The lab at Zaabha wasn't much fun."

His fingers stroked her skin. "You aren't at Zaabha. You're safe."

He stayed close, touching her shoulder as the healers got to work on the implant. She heard the cyborgs talking in clipped tones, and the Hermia healers speaking in their melodious, calm voices.

Sam closed her eyes and tried to drift away. She felt the tugging at her skin, but it didn't hurt. More tugging and her stomach rolled. *Dios*, it felt just like when the Thraxians had put the damn thing in, except she'd been strapped down and screaming.

"Sam." Galen's lips brushed her other temple. "It's almost over."

She wanted to lean into his touch. His voice was enough for her to fight to the surface. She was in the House of Galen. She was safe.

"All finished," Winter said.

"The procedure is complete," came the modulated voice of Garda, the Hermia healer.

"Already?" Sam opened her eyes and saw Galen's rugged face.

He nodded and helped her sit up. "You did great." He glanced at the healers. "I want that implant examined straightaway."

The medical staff all nodded. Galen looked back at Sam and tilted her face up.

"How do you feel?" he asked.

"Better. I'm glad it's over." He stroked her temple and Sam tried to suppress a shiver. "Galen—"

Suddenly, the doors to Medical opened and several House of Galen guards rushed in.

The lead man rested his hand on the hilt of his sheathed sword, his face tense. "Imperator, you're needed."

Galen straightened, and Sam's stomach clenched.

"What's happened?" Galen demanded.

"A riot has broken out at the House of Zeringei, sir," the second guard said. "They're tearing it apart, and everyone is too afraid to help."

CHAPTER SIX

G alen stormed through the corridor, barking orders at his assembling gladiators and guards.

"All right, let's get to the House of Zeringei."

Sam fell into step beside him and he glanced at her. She was wearing fighting leathers, her toned arms on display, and long legs encased in supple, brown leather. The hilt of a sword was visible over her shoulder, sitting snug in the scabbard on her back.

"You're not coming," he ground out.

She lifted her chin, keeping pace with him. "I never signed up for you to give me orders."

"You're House of Galen now."

"Yes, so I'll be a part of this house. And I'll fight when needed."

Galen ground his teeth together. "You just got out of Medical."

"And I'm fine. Over the last few months, I was forced

into the arena battered and bloody. Today, I feel good, and I'm choosing to help."

He stopped and spun to face her, his black cloak flaring out behind him. He sensed his gladiators watching them with avid interest.

Sam stared back at him.

"Fine," he muttered. "Let's go."

A small smile flirted on her lips and she nodded.

As they exited the House of Galen, they broke into a jog, moving through the corridors beneath the arena. As they neared the House of Zeringei, Galen could hear screams and the sound of fighting.

A muscle ticked in his jaw, and he glanced at Raiden. His champion's face was set in hard lines.

Something terrible was happening inside.

Galen looked back at Sam. She looked steady and determined, exactly how her essence felt. He gave them both a short nod and they rounded the final corner.

The large doors into the House of Zeringei were thrown open. He saw several Zeringei gladiators—big, four-armed fighters covered in silver-gray fur—fighting their own people, including innocent, unarmed workers. The gladiators fought brutally, in an uncontrolled frenzy. The tangled mix of essences slammed into him.

There were several bodies littering the floor and, closest to the door, Galen saw a large gladiator raise two swords over a cowering young man.

Galen charged ahead, jamming his own blade against the other gladiator's. He'd replaced the sword he'd lost at Zaabha and he saw the blue-green text flare on the blade.

The Aurelian short sword was his preferred weapon. Spinning, Galen pushed his weight against the gladiator.

"Stand down."

Gaze glittering, the gladiator attacked. Galen cut him down.

Around him, the House of Galen gladiators waded into the fight.

He spotted several workers huddled against the walls. "Get to safety! Lock yourselves in the kitchens."

He spun and saw Sam take down another gladiator. Beyond her, Raiden, Thorin, Kace, and the others were subduing the Zeringei fighters.

It wasn't long until silence fell over the foyer of the House of Zeringei. The out-of-control gladiators were either dead or tied up and on their knees.

"What the *drak* happened here?" Raiden muttered.

"Kace," Galen called out. "Find the Zeringei healers." There were several injured people who needed help.

The gladiator jogged back after a moment. "Dead or injured."

Galen cursed under his breath. "Get back to the House of Galen and send our medical team."

Sam moved up beside Galen. "What a mess."

Galen scanned the bodies on the ground. For a second, he was back on Aurelia, staring at the dead bodies littering the palace.

"Galen."

A slim hand touched his arm, pulling him out of the memories.

"We'll help them rebuild." Beneath the downed body of a fighter, he spotted the large form of the imperator.

He hurried over and dropped to his knee. He pushed the body off the man. "Tano."

"G-Galen," the man croaked. His silver fur was matted with blood.

Galen helped the man up, leaning him against the wall. A huge gash bisected his chest and he was bleeding badly. "We need to get him to Medical."

"Galen." Tano grabbed Galen's arm with two of his hands, his grip weak. "My gladiators...something was wrong. They...went crazy. They're loyal. They wouldn't do this."

Galen nodded. "I'll take care of it, Tano. You need to focus on getting better. Your House needs you."

The imperator slumped back and Galen nodded at Nero. The big gladiator lifted Tano and Lore fell into step beside them. They hurried out the door.

Around Galen, the rest of his gladiators were helping the injured and moving the dead into a side room. Finally, Winter and the House of Galen healers arrived, and quickly set to work.

Galen grimly walked the length of the corridor, studying the dead bodies. Innocent workers, new recruits, and several hardened gladiators who'd fought to protect the others. All dead.

He spotted one gladiator who he recognized from the arena. His long, black hair was a tangled, sweaty mess around his rugged face. A talented fighter who'd been one of Zeringei's best.

Galen crouched, closing the man's sightless eyes.

Galen felt a warmth right behind him and felt Sam's legs brush against his back. She crouched beside him.

"Such a waste." Her sad gaze was on the man's face.

"You've seen a lot of death."

A spasm crossed her face. "Yes. People who should never have been at Zaabha." She squeezed her eyes closed. "People I had to kill."

He gripped her arm and squeezed. "You did what you had to do to survive, Sam."

She nodded. "What happened here?"

"I don't know, but I'm going to find out."

Then Sam frowned and pushed the gladiator's hair off his neck.

That's when Galen saw the tiny, silver circle embedded in the man's skin, just below his ear.

Galen hissed out a sharp breath. "An implant."

It was small. Far smaller than the one they'd removed from Sam today.

"This is much more advanced and sophisticated than any of the ones I've seen."

Galen stood. "This was some kind of test."

Sam rose as well. "A smaller implant is easier to hide."

Anger spiked through him. "They'd better stay out of my city." He turned and punched his fist into the stone wall. The rock cracked. *Drakking Thraxian scum.*

Sam scanned the dead. "Their plans are escalating."

Galen nodded. "And so will ours."

SAM LEAPED OFF THE BED, her fist swinging.

It took her a second to realize there was no Thraxian to fight. And another second to recognize the darkened bedroom.

House of Galen.

She glanced at the timepiece beside her bed and flopped back on her pillows. It had only been thirty minutes since her last nightmare.

Pressing her palms to her eyes, she dragged in some breaths. Her heart was racing, fear clogging her throat. Tears threatened. *No.* She choked them back. Her mother was a crier, and after watching her mother fall apart when Sam's father had been sick, Sam had vowed to not do the same.

Fuck this. She tossed off the covers and strode out of her room. She had no idea where she was going, she just needed to move, to breathe.

After the massacre at the House of Zeringei, Galen had been busy. But he'd come to get her in the afternoon to take her to Zhim's penthouse in the city. The amazing skyscraper wouldn't have looked out of place in Las Vegas. All glitz and glamor. She'd met the happy, energetic Ryan, and the arrogant, interesting Zhim.

And Sam had spoken with her family.

She reached the empty training arena. It was drenched in moonlight and she leaned against one of the pillars. Grief and guilt slammed into her.

Her mother's sobs, the tremor in her father's voice, the sadness in her brothers' words. A cool breeze washed over her, reminding her that she only wore a thin tank and tiny shorts. *Dios*, she missed her family.

Sam fought hard with her conflicting emotions. Her grief at missing them, her guilt because she knew they relied on her, and the pinch of shame that a small part of her didn't miss their neediness. *Dios*, it was part of the reason she'd gone to Fortuna. But it didn't matter that they sometimes drove her crazy, she loved them.

She closed her eyes, but there was no relief there either. Her nightmares came back to her: the faces of the fighters she'd been forced to kill, the ragged pain of injuries, and the helplessness of being trapped. No better than a wild dog forced to fight.

"Sam."

His deep voice came from the darkness.

"I'm fine." *Go away, please.* She didn't want him to see her break.

His arm brushed against hers. He stood beside her in silence.

She swallowed, staring across the arena at the guards patrolling on the far side. "You have a gap in your security by the wall there. Someone could scale it and get in if they know the guard patrol rosters."

Galen studied the wall for a moment. "You're right. I'll take care of it."

Now, go. Her nails bit into her palms.

But he didn't. Instead, he stared up at the night sky. "The city lights drown out most of the stars, but you can still see the brightest ones."

Blinking back the tears she didn't want to let fall, she looked up.

"That large one over there is called *Neridae*." He

pointed. "The smaller cluster just over the wall is called the Dancing Sisters."

"I'm about to break, Galen. Please, leave me alone."

He turned to her. "So break. You're entitled."

"I can't." Her hands curled tighter. "I have to be strong and hold it together."

"Why?"

"Because I always have to. There's no one to catch me if I fall." There hadn't been when her father was sick, nor at Zaabha. "I'm not sure I can pick up the pieces."

Strong arms wrapped around her and pulled her close. Warmth pumped off him and she almost moaned. She gripped his biceps, holding on tight.

"There are lots of people around you, Sam, and they're all holding out a hand. After everything, you're entitled to purge the hurt inside you. It's okay to lean."

She saw his face in the shadows, the rugged line of his jaw. "If I break, the pieces may never go back together."

"Sure they will. There will just be scars."

She lifted a hand and stroked the scar bisecting his left eye. "Is it easy to live with the scars?"

"Mine are far uglier than yours will ever be, Sam."

She saw the dead in her head, heard their screams and pleas. "I don't believe that." Her voice broke.

He pressed her face to his chest. "Let go. I've got you."

A man who always kept his promises, and yet, still punished himself for the ones he'd failed to fulfill.

A tear slid down her cheek, followed by a sob.

Galen smoothed a hand up her back. "There you go. It's okay, Sam. You aren't alone."

She broke, the cries ripping from her. She cried for what she'd lost, the people she'd killed, the pain she'd suffered and inflicted. She cried until she sagged against him, exhausted and empty.

There wasn't pain anymore. There was nothing.

Galen dipped and lifted her off her feet. She was too tired to put up a protest.

When he laid her on the bed and started to pull away, she gripped him. "Stay."

He hesitated.

She swallowed, her eyes feeling swollen. She couldn't make herself ask again.

He didn't say anything, just lay on top of the covers beside her and pulled her close.

She'd broken, but somehow Galen had kept all her pieces together. With his strong arms around her, and his scent deep in her senses, she fell into a dreamless sleep.

SAM SWUNG THE STAFF, feet shifting on the sand. It hit against Kace's staff with a *thwack,* and she felt the power of the blow vibrate up her arms.

She stepped back, eyeing her opponents. Kace and Saff stood across from her in the training arena, both holding their staffs up. Kace's face was serious and composed, and Saff was grinning.

Sam moved in again, spinning and ducking. She

thrust the staff out. Her muscles were warm, and it was actually nice to spar for fun and exercise.

Kace met her strike and Saff spun, kicking up sand.

Sam leaped back. Here, she could enjoy the sunshine on her face, the pump of adrenaline in her blood, and the challenge of fighting two skilled gladiators.

She attacked again, dropped low and swept her weapon out. As expected, Kace jumped, but Sam moved upward, following him and managed to hit his shins. With a curse, he tripped.

As the big gladiator fell in the sand, Saff leaped over him, rushing at Sam. Sam stepped back, widened her stance, then dropped her staff. She ducked Saff's weapon, gripped the woman's leathers, and flipped the female gladiator over her shoulder.

Saff landed flat on her back on the sand. She pushed up on her elbows. "You fight mean."

"I had to." Sam straightened. "Or I'd be dead."

Once, she'd been a by-the-book fighter. She'd joined the military right out of school, followed by a short stint with the International Marshals Service before she'd joined Fortuna Station. She'd been filled with a need to help others, fight for the less fortunate, and help bring justice to those in need.

But Zaabha had taught her that sometimes you had to fight dirty to win the day.

Saff rose, respect in her eyes. "Not anymore."

Kace was back on his feet and he touched Sam's shoulder gently, but didn't say anything.

Sam felt the burn of tears in her eyes. *Dios*, she never

cried. *Well, you fell apart last night.* She'd cried all over Galen and then slept in his arms.

When she'd woken from the best sleep she'd had since her abduction, Galen had been gone, just leaving his scent and an imprint on the pillow behind.

Saff and Kace both straightened and turned. She followed their gaze and her breath caught in her chest.

It shouldn't. It wasn't like she hadn't seen the man move before.

Galen strode across the sand, that black cloak of his flaring out behind him. He didn't move with any swagger, like some of the other gladiators. Every step was contained power.

Something inside Sam quivered just looking at him, and she admitted to herself that she *really* wanted to tear the man's cloak and leathers off. She wanted to touch his skin and make his heart beat faster.

"We have a meeting." Galen's icy gaze swept over them before settling on Sam. It skimmed over her, as if he was assessing how she was. "Rillian and Zhim are here."

"They have information on the implants?" Kace asked.

Galen nodded.

Sam moved with Saff and Kace to set their staffs on the racks. Several workers were there, cleaning and maintaining other weapons. As always, it was another clear reminder that Galen ran his house well.

They moved through the doorway, and she took a second to adjust from the bright sunshine to the shadowed interior. Galen moved quickly, and they followed him into the living area of the high-level gladiators.

The long table was packed with Galen's gladiators and all the women.

At the far end, Sam saw Rillian and Dayna, and nodded at the couple. In the kitchen, she spotted a small woman with straight, black hair and some Japanese heritage. She was stirring something in a mug, and appeared to be bickering with the tall, lean, dark-haired man beside her. She'd met computer expert Ryan Nagano and information merchant, Zhim when she'd spoken with her family.

Kace and Saff sat, while Galen moved to stand at the head of the table. Sam took the seat to Galen's left. Ryan and Zhim moved to join them.

"Rillian," Galen said. "You have information for us."

The casino owner nodded. "I've been tapping all my contacts. The Thraxians are in the city."

There were hisses and grunts around the table.

"But they're laying low and staying quiet," Rillian continued. "I haven't got a single hint of what they're doing or what they have planned."

Sam tensed. They knew the Thraxians were planning something, and her gut knew they were beginning to put whatever it was into play.

Zhim stood, pressing his hands to the table. "Ryan and I found nothing about the Thraxian implants anywhere on the system. We searched everywhere." The man's frustration was evident.

Ryan reached up, her fingers closing around Zhim's arm. "My guess is that the Thraxians aren't linking the implant data to the system. I knew their system at Zaabha pretty well, and I know the lab had a discrete system."

Sam leaned forward. "I saw the data crystal the lead Thraxian scientist kept in his lab. A cube, of some sort. He bragged about it containing all his data."

Galen looked at her. "You're sure that all the implant information is on the crystal?"

She nodded. "Yes. And it's stored in his lab."

"Everything keeps coming back to the damn implants." Galen looked around the table. "The Thraxians tested their new implants on the House of Zeringei and slaughtered innocents."

Shocked silence fell, but Sam felt the anger vibrating around the room.

"I want the medical team to speed up their examination of the implants," Galen ordered. "We also have the ones from the Zeringei gladiators, in addition to the ones taken from Sam and Ever. We need to know everything about them."

Winter nodded from where she sat close beside her gladiator, Nero. "We're working on it. We've discovered data on Sam's implant and we're trying to access it."

"Work with Magnus' people." Galen looked each one of them in the eye. "Until we know more, there's nothing we can do...yet. For now, we keep trying to find out exactly what the Thraxians have planned, and what their use of these implants means."

"We won't let them win," Raiden said.

With that, everyone in the room dispersed, and Sam found herself mobbed by her friends. Out of the corner of her eye, she saw Galen slip out with his gladiators.

When she finally broke free of the women, she headed down the corridor. When she reached the door to

Galen's office, she pressed her shoulder against the door jamb. "So, this is your domain."

He looked up from his desk. He looked every inch the in-charge imperator.

"This is where I work."

Where he ran his House, trained exceptional gladiators, and took care of those he considered his. She strode in, feeling restless.

He watched her for a second. "What do you need, Sam?"

"You're good at that." She turned to study him. "Good at working out what people need and giving it to them."

"That's how I was raised." A pause. "I can see you're uneasy, so, what do you need?"

She lifted a shoulder. "I'm not sure. I just feel so damn helpless, sitting around waiting and trying to adjust to being free." She moved closer, hitching her hip on the edge of his desk. "I'm used to action."

"I know. I want to stop the Thraxians as much as you do."

She scraped a hand through her hair. "It's hard... going from captivity to freedom."

"Healing takes time. I've watched the other humans begin to bloom as days pass. You need to give yourself a break."

She sighed. "I know."

"I also watched Raiden mourn for his family and our world. Even after we made a new life for ourselves, he wasn't truly complete until Harper came into his world."

Sam tilted her head. "What about you?"

"What do you mean?"

"Have you healed?"

His jaw went tight. "My job was to protect the royal family, my planet, and my fellow royal guards. I failed them all."

"Your job was to protect your prince. You did that."

"And now I ensure that Raiden thrives."

Without living himself. It sounded like classic survivor's guilt to her. "Not anymore, Galen. Raiden's no longer your prince, no longer your teenage charge. He and his happiness aren't your job anymore."

She saw him scowl, and Sam wondered just what it would take for Galen to put his own needs first.

"Aren't you allowed to enjoy yourself?" she asked.

"I'm too busy."

Then she had an idea. She straightened. "I've thought of something I want."

"What?"

"I want to cook."

CHAPTER SEVEN

It felt so good to be doing something she loved again.

Sam moved the pan over the heat. She had ingredients spread all over the counter tops. Most of them were strange and wonderful. The House of Galen chefs had looked shocked when she and Galen had first arrived in the kitchens. The head chef himself had helped her select equipment and ingredients—ones he knew were friendly to a human palate. Then the kitchen staff had disappeared to give her some privacy.

And right now, she was smiling and felt relaxed. She thought of her *mamá*—Dolores, known as Lola to her family—and knew she'd be happy Sam was cooking.

Galen had watched Sam for a while with a bemused expression. He'd explained a few of the fruits and vegetables to her, including pointing out the *fidea* he loved, before he'd finally headed back to his office for a meeting.

She reached for a bowl and stirred it. A cloud of... well, she was calling it flour, but who knew exactly what it came from, puffed into the air. After Galen had left, she'd tracked the chef down again and asked him a few questions.

Sam wiggled her hips, imagining the music that her mother liked to listen to when she cooked was playing. She was going to have to ask Mia for some music, next time. She remembered her nieces' giggles whenever they'd cooked together. The girls would probably be taller now. It felt like a lifetime ago since she'd seen them.

And now she never would.

The sharp pain made her bite her lip and her hand clenched on the utensil. Closing her eyes, Sam let the ache wash through her until it finally dulled enough that she could breathe.

She knew the loss of her family would hurt for the rest of her life, but she had to find a way to deal with it. For now, she was going to focus on cooking a meal for a man she suspected never let anyone take care of him.

When the food was ready, she dished it onto plates she'd rested on a tray. She'd wanted to make her favorite *pasteles*, but trying to find a substitute for banana leaves to wrap the pastries had proved too difficult on a desert planet. The chef had told her a trip to the underground market would be necessary. She'd made *arroz mamposteao* with meat and beans instead. Okay, it was sort of like rice, and the beans were...not quite the same as beans, but close. She'd had to substitute everything. She had no idea what animal the meat had come from, but the chef had assured her that when he served it to Galen, his plate always came back empty. She'd experimented with spices and taste-tested everything. It was all pretty darn good.

For dessert, she'd attempted to make *tembleque*. Her *mamá* would probably be horrified at the result, because it wasn't quite the same as the coconut pudding her mother made. But after several failed experiments, Sam had managed to make a sweet-tasting dessert she hoped Galen liked.

She pulled a final tray out of the oven. Her *pan de Mallorca* looked pretty darn good. The Puerto Rican sweet rolls were her secret addiction. She placed a few of the rolls on a plate.

Holding the tray, she left the kitchen and made her way up to Galen's office.

She passed some young gladiator recruits, who nodded at her. She smiled back. The recruits looked fit and healthy, and well-equipped with staffs and axes. She realized she liked the House of Galen. Quite a bit. She liked the solid, stone walls, and the gorgeous wall hangings, depicting battles in the arena. There was a sense of history here, more evidence that Galen ran his house well.

When she reached his office, she saw his head bent over his desk as he read something. His brow was furrowed.

Did the man take any time off?

Sam sauntered in and his gaze flicked up. For a second, her mind went blank. *Dios*, he was something to look at. Not handsome, but something beyond that—tough, rugged, and strong. Strength radiated off him, and made you know that he'd shield you and keep you safe.

"Dinner is served."

He raised a brow.

She set the tray down on his desk. "*Arroz mamposteao,* a sort of fried rice with meat and whatever those things are." She pointed at her bean substitute. "And for dessert, my own version of *tembleque.* A sweet treat my *mamá* makes. Plus a few Puerto Rican sweet rolls."

He eyed it all. "You cooked for me."

"I promise there isn't any poison in there." She perched on the edge of his desk.

He grabbed a utensil and tried some rice. His eye widened.

She laughed. "Were you expecting it to be bad?"

"I had no idea." He scooped up some more, trying the meat. He smiled, clearly liking it.

Sam liked seeing that smile. He was pretty stingy with them.

His gaze traced her face. "You have so many facets. I can't seem to get a handle on any of them. I expected a battle-hardened warrior."

"I'm that."

"I didn't expect a gourmet chef."

"I think gourmet is stretching it."

As he tried some of the dessert, she saw the faintest flutter of his eyelid. Hmm, the workaholic imperator had a sweet tooth. As he took another spoonful, she felt a spike of satisfaction. She liked watching him enjoy himself and relax a little. He also ate more than one of her sweet rolls.

"What are you working on?" she asked.

"I'm going over everything I have on the Thraxians, and all the information I've accumulated on Zaabha."

Her muscles tensed. "Tell me."

They talked about the implants and Thraxians. He spun the screen around so she could see the data.

"What the hell are they planning, Galen?"

He grabbed her hand. "I wish I knew. But we *will* stop them. We will take them down."

She linked her fingers with his, feeling his calluses brush her skin. "I know."

The air felt charged and their gazes locked.

He cleared his throat. "I have some House business to attend to."

"Let me help."

He studied her for a second, then nodded. She pulled a chair around the desk, and watched as he pulled out some paper files. Carthago was such a perplexing mix of low and high tech, and she found that fact strangely amusing and endearing.

Galen started going through inventory issues and training schedules. Sam offered some suggestions, and they talked about several improvements. For a moment, she felt she was back on Fortuna Station, locked in her office and working on her security paperwork.

She watched him take a bite of another sweet roll and hid her smile. "I'd really like to go over your training schedules." She leaned over and pointed at the chart. "I was watching your recruits train, and I have some ideas."

He nodded. "I'm sure my recruits and trainers would benefit from any advice from the Champion of Zaabha."

Sam felt a warmth rush through her. She could add

value here. "I had some ideas for how you could mix up the weapons training." She walked him through her thoughts.

He grunted. "That's an excellent suggestion."

She looked up and smiled. Then she stilled. Their faces were close together.

"You smile more than I guessed you would," he said, after a long moment. "After what you've been through."

"Being the boss, or having gone through a hard time, doesn't mean you have to be serious all the time, Galen." She reached out, gently rubbing the groove in the center of his brow.

A strong hand reached up and gripped her wrist. Then he turned her hand over, studying her palm.

"Such elegant hands." He stroked her skin "Strong enough to wield a sword, talented enough to cook an exceptional meal." He leaned down and pressed a kiss to the center of her palm.

Sam shuddered, her gaze glued to him. She thought she saw surprise on his face. Surprise he'd initiated such an intimate gesture.

His lips moved up to her fingers. His tongue darted out, licking between the digits. Sam's belly tumbled with the zing of pleasure and anticipation.

"I can taste the dessert you made me."

"I may have tested it."

"Sweet." He licked again.

Sam couldn't help it, she moaned.

He stilled, his face hardening. "I'm trying to stay away from you." The words were a growl.

"Why?"

"You need time and space to heal."

"That's nice, Galen, but unnecessary." She cocked her head. "Don't you ever just do something spontaneous? Something you want?"

"No."

She shifted closer to him. "You're allowed pleasure, Galen."

His gaze dropped to her mouth. The icy blue of his eye glittered with heat. "I've never wanted something so badly before."

Desire hit her, coiling low in her belly. She leaned closer to him.

The knock at the door made them both jerk apart.

"Excuse me, Imperator." Two guards stepped inside, both wearing red-and-gray cloaks, with swords sheathed at their hips. "We're here for the evening security report."

"Duty calls." Sam sat back, her heart beating hard. Ignoring the guards, she reached up and stroked Galen's stubbled jaw. "I'll let you get back to your work. I'll see you later, Galen."

She felt his gaze on her as she walked out. The sensation put a smile on her face.

LATE THE NEXT MORNING, Galen found Sam going over training plans with Kace.

"Sam?"

She spun, shooting him a smile. "Hi."

Need slammed into him and he beat it back. "I had word from Magnus. They found something."

Her smile dissolved, her face turning serious. "What?"

"Magnus told me he'd tell us when we get to the House of Rone." Galen took her arm and nodded at Kace. "We'll update everyone when we get back."

Together, he and Sam strode out of the House of Galen. He tried not to notice the way her leather trousers hugged her form. Or how her thick, brown-gold hair was pulled back in a long tail that fell past her shoulders.

"You're sure we can trust the cyborgs?"

"Yes," he replied. "The House of Rone is our ally. Magnus is an honorable man."

Sam released a breath. "Sorry. I saw too many augmented fighters at Zaabha. None of them were very friendly or honorable."

Galen touched her arm. They continued down the tunnels, and soon turned another corner. The doors of the House of Rone were ahead, with the House logo embossed on it—a gladiator helmet resting on crossed swords. Cyborg guards flanked the doors, and Galen nodded at them. They silently opened the doors.

"Sam." Ever rushed forward to give Sam a hug.

Magnus was just behind her, his face cool, and his muscled body clothed in black. He was holding a sleeping baby in the crook of his arm.

Galen shook his head. There was a sight he'd never thought to see. A huge, seemingly emotionless cyborg carting a baby around like it was the most precious thing he'd ever seen.

As Galen watched, Sam moved forward and gently stroked the baby's cheek.

Something shifted inside of Galen. *What the drak?* He'd never given any thought to kids. Protecting Raiden had been his life, his duty.

But watching Sam bend over that small baby... He frowned.

"Let's talk in the main hall," Magnus said.

They went inside and sat down on some couches.

"Winter and the healers sent your implant to us, Sam," Ever said.

"We've also been studying several of the smaller implants from the House of Zeringei," Magnus added.

Ever leaned forward. "These newer implants are fascinating, and the Thraxians have made remarkable improvements. The implant is smaller and more powerful."

"What did you find?" Galen demanded.

Ever shared a look with Magnus. "We found a blueprint in the data."

"About how to make the implants?" Sam asked.

"No." Magnus' voice was ice cold. "The Thraxians plan to infiltrate the Kor Magna Arena."

Galen frowned. "What?"

"They want to rule it," Ever said.

"The imperators rule the arena," Galen said.

"The Thraxians want to implant gladiators and control all the Houses." Now Magnus' tone vibrated with anger. "They want to rig the fights to make more money."

Sam shook her head and Galen felt his own fury boil up inside him.

"Sand-sucking cowards," he snapped.

"Galen." Magnus stared at him and Galen saw the glimmer of rage. "We have to stop this."

Before Ever, Magnus had shown very little emotion, but since the cyborg had fallen in love, he showed glimpses of emotion more freely.

Sam's hand fisted and she bumped it on her leg. "This is bigger than just Zaabha."

"Zaabha was their testing ground," Ever said quietly.

Galen gritted his teeth. "This is war."

Magnus nodded. "War."

Sam reached out and squeezed Galen's thigh. That touch helped him find some control.

"What do we do next?" she asked.

"I'm going to call a meeting of all the Houses and their imperators. Next, we put our army together."

She nodded, her face calm and composed. He wasn't looking at the smiling woman who'd cooked for him, or the interested woman who helped him with House business. This was the battle-hardened warrior.

Sam stood. "Then we go to war."

CHAPTER EIGHT

A s they walked through the tunnels heading back to the House of Galen, Sam could see that Galen was lost in thought and brooding. His hard jaw was tight, and that groove in his brow was back.

Part of her wanted to help him. Made her want to give something to him, and see him relax and smile. She knew he was angry about the Thraxians and their plan. She felt the same.

And that feeling wouldn't go away until they stopped the bastards.

When they reached the House of Galen, he stormed off without a word. She stared at his back as he strode away.

"He gets like this sometimes." Raiden stood beside her. "Holes up, broods for a while. Best to give him some time."

As Raiden walked away, Sam stared at the empty corridor Galen had used. He had no one to talk to, lean

IMPERATOR

on, who worried about him. His people saw him as strong and unbending.

Sam saw beneath to the man.

Galen was just so used to being alone that he never asked for help. She turned and walked down the corridor. At the end was the door to his private suite. Two guards flanked it—one older with an experienced look in his eye and the second a young recruit.

As she drew near, the guards shifted, crossing their staffs to block her way.

She looked at them. "That's not going to stop me."

"The imperator doesn't want to be disturbed," the younger man said.

"Well, the imperator is used to getting what he wants and not enough of what he needs," Sam responded.

The older guard eyed her with a considering look. She took another step and the recruit tensed.

The older man shook his head. "You can't take her, boy. She'd leave you bleeding and use your hide for fighting leathers. Let her pass." He pulled his staff away from the door.

The young guard stared a moment longer, then reluctantly stepped back.

As Sam walked past them, the older man gave her a faint smile. She nodded at him and walked through the door.

"Mistress Sam?"

She looked back. The young recruit met her gaze, but looked ready to fidget. "I heard you might start training sessions with the new recruits." He lifted his chin. "I'd like to be a part of your training."

Feeling lodged in her throat, but she kept her face steady. "I'll expect to see you there, recruit."

He lowered his head and Sam let the door close.

She moved through the large, spacious living area. It was clearly a man's domain, decorated in shades of black and gray with the odd touch of blue and red. A set of carved stairs led to an upper level that she guessed was his bedroom. The arched doors to the terrace were open.

She stepped out into a small, private training arena. It was bathed in golden light from the afternoon sun. *Dios*, she loved it. Dark green vines grew up the surrounding stone walls.

But as her gaze shifted, all she saw was the man.

Galen swung his sword with powerful flexes of muscle. He wore no shirt or cloak. He was only clad in well-worn leather trousers, a simple leather harness, and gauntlets on his forearms. His muscles gleamed.

He moved with formidable confidence, his powerful blows tearing open the training dummy. The script on his sword flared, and for a second, she thought she saw his tattoos glow too. When she blinked, she only saw black ink and figured she'd imagined it.

She strode across the sand and saw Galen pause, lowering his sword. His back was to her.

"I want to be alone." His voice was deep and gritty.

Sí, definitely brooding. He was so tense, his back muscles taut. He carried so much weight on his broad shoulders.

"I think you're too used to being left alone," she said. "Drowning in your guilt."

He spun, a muscle ticking on his unsmiling face. "Leave."

She crossed her arms over her chest. "No."

His eye widened. She suspected that was a word Galen wasn't used to hearing.

"You helped me the other night," she said. "You held me together when everything was too much. I want to help you. I want you to relax."

He didn't move. "I should have stopped the Thraxians a long time ago."

"None of this is your fault, Galen. The blame lies solely with the Thraxians, for all the atrocities they've committed. Including the destruction of your planet."

He spun and threw his sword. The blade speared the training dummy through its faceless head, setting it rocking.

"I don't need any help."

Stubborn man. She strode to the small weapons rack at the side of the arena. She barely swallowed her moan of appreciation. It was filled with the highest quality swords of all shapes and sizes.

She lifted a sword similar to the one she'd used before. She liked the size and weight of it, and when her fingers curled around the hilt, she saw inscriptions gleam on the metal.

"An Aurelian short sword," Galen said.

He'd retrieved his own sword and she saw the matching inscriptions on it. "From your homeworld?"

"Yes. The script is a verse to honor the warrior, to give them strength and skill in battle."

She raised the sword. If he wouldn't talk, she had

another idea for how to get him to burn off his tension. "So, are you up for a challenge, Imperator Galen?"

"I don't want to fight you."

"Not afraid of the Champion of Zaabha, are you?" She jabbed, her sword missing his face by an inch.

He didn't move, didn't flinch. "Sam." A warning tone.

She used the tip of her sword to lift his up. "Come on, Galen. Show me what you've got."

He exploded into action.

Sam danced backward, meeting his blows. She ducked and dodged, spinning around his body. She struck back, and he met her, hit for hit. He deflected her strikes or met them with hard swings of his own.

It wasn't long before her arms were burning. They moved back across the small arena, turned, and kept fighting.

It felt almost like a dance—a fast, deadly one.

When Galen finally stepped back, the sunlight was long gone. The shadows were broken only by the glow of orange lights that had come on. Chest burning, Sam leaned over, pressing her hands to her thighs.

"Not bad," she said.

Galen raised a brow. She could tell not all the tension was gone, but it was a start. "Why do I get the feeling you wanted to add 'for an old man' to that?"

She smiled. "You said it, not me."

He grunted, placing his sword on the rack. He moved over to a large chair set up beside a small table. A long cool drink rested there...as well as a plate of her sweet rolls.

A pleasant clench in her belly. He dropped into the

chair and lifted the glass. As he drank the liquid, she watched his strong throat work. Desire curled inside her. *Dios*, the man was attractive.

"You like my sweet rolls?" she said.

"Yes." He set the glass down. "Thanks for checking on me. You can go now."

Ow, she'd been dismissed. But as she stared at that blue eye that looked like cut glass, she still saw the boiling emotions—anger, guilt, fury, pain—before he hid them.

Luckily, Sam didn't scare easily. She sauntered toward him.

GALEN SAT IN HIS CHAIR, willing Sam to leave.

Instead, the infuriating woman moved closer. He smelled her scent, something spicy covered in healthy sweat.

He wanted to be alone. He was feeling on edge, the jagged void inside him extra hungry tonight. On nights like this, he locked himself away until the worst of his bad mood was gone.

"I'm starting to think you have no idea what the word 'relax' means." She lifted his glass and took a sip.

There was something incredibly intimate about the move and his gaze locked on her. The muscles in his body were stretched tight.

She moved behind him and a second later, he felt her working the buckle of his harness loose.

"Sam—"

"Just be quiet, Galen. Relax."

He let out a breath. The quickest way to get her to leave was to let her finish. She nudged him forward and pulled his harness off. Next, she lifted his right arm, freeing his gauntlet, then his left arm.

When she slipped behind him again, he wasn't sure what to expect. Her hands on his shoulders burned through his skin.

Then she started to knead the muscles in his neck and shoulders.

Drak. He swallowed a groan, his head falling forward. She had strong fingers and seemed to know exactly where to press.

She massaged his shoulders, her touch so good. Then she moved up his neck, working deep, and finding several knots that she gave her attention.

Galen felt the tension slowly seep out of him, his muscles relaxing one by one. Her hands moved up into his scalp and he bit back a groan. Her fingers brushed his eyepatch.

"There, that feels better, doesn't it?" Her voice was low.

He cleared his throat. He felt better physically, but inside, he still felt the throb of anger, still felt that horrible darkness that always haunted him and scraped him raw. It had reminded him that he could never truly relax, never let up. Your enemies were always waiting to strike.

"Yes, thank you." He paused. "Sam...I will do everything I can to help you make a life here. You deserve it."

She stepped in front of him. "But?"

"I'm not a part of that life, except as your imperator."

She tensed. "You're going to deny that we're attracted to each other?"

"No. But I have nothing to offer you. You need a man who...can love you the right way. That isn't and will never be me."

Her lip trembled before she firmed it. "The great Galen won't risk falling in love." There was a hard bite in her voice.

"I was bred never to love." The words shot out of him. "I don't have it in me."

She leaned forward. "You won't let yourself. It's all part of your self-imposed punishment for things that were never your fault."

He stiffened. "You talk of things that you don't understand."

She threw her hands up. "You know what, you're right. I do deserve a man who'll love me. Who'll take me as I am. Who'll let me help him shoulder his burden. A man who isn't a coward." Her chest hitched. "A man who wants me enough that he..." Her voice cracked. "I'm done with men who want parts of me, but not all of me." She spun to leave.

Galen's arm shot out and he gripped her wrist. His gut was churning. The thought of any man not wanting her was inconceivable. And the thought of some other, faceless man touching her, loving her... A bitter taste climbed his throat.

Their gazes locked, but he couldn't make himself say anything.

Sam shook her head. "I always seem to be attracted to

men who don't want me enough." She yanked out of his hold and walked away, head held high.

Not want her enough? Galen gripped the armrests of his chair hard enough that they creaked. He realized that strong, proud Sam had been hurt by men in her past.

And in trying to protect her, he'd added to that pain.

He blew out a breath, sitting there in the darkness. The realization hit him that he was protecting himself as much as her.

She was right. He was a coward. Caring hurt. Loving hurt. Especially when you failed and the things you loved were taken away.

CHAPTER NINE

S am waited for Galen at the front doors of the House
of Galen.

He'd sent a message via a House worker that he was
meeting with a difficult imperator today—Imperator
Mortas of the House of Mortas—prior to the larger
meeting with all the imperators. He'd invited her to
join him.

She wasn't sure why he'd invited her. An apology?
Extending an offer of friendship?

Sam wasn't sure she could be Galen's friend.

She hadn't slept that well, and this time she couldn't
blame the Thraxians. She'd tossed in her sheets, unable
to sleep.

Her fight with Galen—both the physical one and the
emotional one—had left her upset and drained.

And despite the ache in her chest, she hadn't
forgotten about touching him...all those hard muscles.
She blew out a breath. Feeling him melt under her touch

was sexy as hell. Lying in her bed, her body had been too turned on. She'd finally had to touch herself and bring herself to climax. But Galen had followed her into her dreams.

For the first time in her life, she'd found a man who attracted her on so many different levels. But who didn't want her enough to open himself up.

She heard footsteps and looked up. Her chest locked.

He strode closer, those thick, muscular legs encased in leather, his black cloak flaring behind him.

His ice-blue gaze was on her, and Sam had to force herself to stay where she was.

"*Buenos días,*" he murmured.

Her eyes widened. "*Buenos días.* Who taught you that?"

"I have my ways." He nodded at the guards to open the doors. "Are you ready for the meeting?"

"Meeting with a hostile imperator who's arrogant and pompous? Walk in the park."

Galen snorted. "I assume walking in the park is an Earth term."

"Right. I mean it's easy, no problem."

They moved into the tunnel outside the House of Galen. She didn't pretend not to feel the tension quivering between them. The tunnels were quiet, only a few arena workers hurrying along, carrying out their business. As they walked, she saw the way people deferred to Galen—nods, smiles, or moving quickly out of his way.

The man was far too used to people complying. He definitely needed someone to shake him up a bit.

She was so lost in her own thoughts, that she was unprepared for the attack.

A huge explosion rocked the tunnel, and the wall beside them collapsed.

Rock and debris hit her. She was knocked off her feet, a large stone hitting her in the chest and winding her.

With her ears ringing, Sam sat up, coughing. Dust filled the air. She saw Galen down on one knee, blood streaming down his face. He reached over his shoulder and drew his sword. A scary look settled on his face.

What could he see? She frowned and heard the deep thud of running footsteps. She guessed he sensed the essences of whoever was incoming.

Several Thraxians ran through the hole in the wall.

Fuck. The aliens rushed at Galen. He swung his sword, surging to his feet.

Sam tried to stand and draw her own sword, but dizziness washed over her. *Dammit.* She managed to get up and lift her weapon, just as a Thraxian rushed at her.

She heaved with all her might. The Thraxian ducked, but she was ready with a kick that pushed him back. She spun and saw another Thraxian bearing down on her. He was big, with massive, black horns, and holding a giant axe.

He swung the weapon. Sam dodged and her shoulder slammed into the wall.

The axe embedded into the wall right beside her. With a shout, the Thraxian yanked it out and swung again.

Sam leaped backward, but her foot hit rubble and she

went down. She looked up and saw the axe descending right at her.

Shit. Suddenly, Galen leaped into view. He sliced his sword through the air, cutting into the Thraxian's axe arm.

The axe clattered to the floor and the Thraxian staggered, holding his wounded arm to his chest. More Thraxians rushed at them.

Blood pumping, Sam swiveled onto hands and knees and pushed to her feet. She had to help Galen.

A clawed hand sank into her hair and wrenched her head back. She gritted her teeth against the pain.

Struggling, she tried to kick the Thraxian holding her. "Come on, you coward."

Then she felt a sharp sting at the side of her neck.

What the hell? Instantly, her limbs relaxed, and her heartrate slowed. She blinked slowly, warmth suffusing her. *No. No. No.*

She knew the sensation. She knew the drug was the one the Thraxians used to make difficult Zaabha prisoners more compliant.

Her sword fell to the ground. She tried to fight the effects, but she could only scream inside her head, and her body was just a limp rag. The Thraxian started dragging her down the tunnel, her feet bumping over the debris.

She managed to lift her head and saw Galen with his back to her, fighting the other Thraxians.

"Galen." In her head it was a shout, but she knew it came out no more than a whisper.

Still, his head swiveled. That single eye focused on her.

His face hardened and he hit at his opponents, fighting to get to her. He let out a roar that echoed off the tunnel.

Sam did a slow blink. *Dios*, he was something.

But then the Thraxian holding her dragged her around a corner and she lost sight of Galen. They moved through a maze of empty tunnels and a second later, sunlight speared into her eyes. She blinked again.

They were in the arena.

"Back to Zaabha for you," the Thraxian growled.

No. Sam's heart clenched hard. She couldn't go back.

She tried to fight against the drug. She wouldn't go back. *Ever.*

He ignored her struggles and pushed her down onto the sand-covered arena. A shadow passed overhead and Sam looked up. There was something in the sky.

Her heart started a loud pound in her ears. A ship was lowering down into the center of the arena floor.

She knew instantly that it was a Zaabha ship. It looked like a smaller version of the Zaabha arena platform, with smoke bellowing out the back of it. It was one of the shuttles they used to transport spectators to Zaabha.

She felt so horribly alone. She felt like the House of Galen was just a dream, one that had been snatched away. Once again, she only had herself to depend on.

Come on, Sam. She swung wildly, slamming a punch into the Thraxian's side. It was weak and ineffectual, and all the alien did was laugh.

The ship hovered just above them, kicking up the sand in a cloud. Sam closed her eyes as grains peppered her skin.

Focus.

She opened her eyes to squint, and saw a large knife hanging off the Thraxian's belt. She reached for it and missed. Gritting her teeth, she reached again, and her hand closed on the hilt. She yanked it off his belt.

"Hey." The Thraxian turned.

With all her strength, she drove her elbow into the Thraxian's gut and managed to rip herself free of his hold. She backed up and lifted the knife. She was unsteady on her feet, and her vision was blurry, but she wasn't going back to Zaabha.

The Thraxian looked at her, baring ugly, black teeth. "You think you can take me?"

"I'm the Champion of Zaabha."

"You're our property," he spat.

"Fuck you. I'm Samantha Santos and no one owns me." She took a step forward and raised the knife.

He smirked at her, but then his eyes widened with fear.

Sam frowned, a bit surprised considering she was weaving like a drunk, but when his gaze moved over her shoulder, she knew that he wasn't looking at her.

She turned her head to look for herself. Galen was running toward them across the sand, his black cloak flaring out behind him. He was covered in blood and grime, his face set and scary.

And the tattoos on his skin were glowing a bright blue-green.

She sucked in a breath. Hope, relief, and a jumble of other unidentifiable emotions ran through her. She took another deep, calming breath.

"Oh, and asshole?" She turned back to the Thraxian. "I'm also House of Galen."

Sam launched forward, slashing with the knife.

The Thraxian yelled. She drew blood on his chest before his clawed hand smacked into her shoulder, knocking her back. Galen leaped over her, his sword driving into the Thraxian's belly.

Losing her balance, Sam fell down on the sand on one knee. But she didn't care. She was smiling, because she wasn't going back to Zaabha, and she knew for sure that she was no longer alone.

IT HAD BEEN a long time since Galen had felt fear. Right now, it churned inside him with his anger.

When he'd lost sight of Sam, knowing they were taking her again, he'd felt fear he hadn't felt since his boots were last on Aurelian soil.

He yanked his sword free of the Thraxian's gut. He saw the Thraxian ship had landed, just sitting on the sand ahead of them. "Sam."

"Here. I'm okay."

He took her in, emotion sweeping through him. She was down on one knee, wavering a little. Battered, but alive.

She blinked slowly. "They drugged me."

That's when Galen noticed that her brown eyes were unfocused. Sand suckers.

Then her face changed. "Galen!"

He spun and saw five Thraxians step off the ship. Everything inside him went icy-cold. He gripped Sam's arm and helped her to her feet, grimly watching the newcomers.

"Stay back," he warned her.

Sam snorted. "Yeah, right."

He shook his head, watching as she lifted the knife with a shaky hand.

Stubborn and determined. "You're drugged, so please stay back." A wry smile flickered over his lips. "I'll take care of them."

Turning, he strode toward the Thraxians.

"We'll grind you and your house to dust," the lead Thraxian shouted.

"You can try."

Galen had never been one to waste time with taunts. He launched forward to attack, swinging his sword.

The next two minutes became a series of lunges, swings, and turns. Energy filled him, his tattoos glowing, signifying his status as a royal bodyguard. They enhanced his strength, giving him a punch of energy and speed. They hadn't glowed since Raiden had become an adult.

Galen cut one Thraxian down and another charged at him. Galen spun and thrust. Then he turned, slamming his elbow into the face of another Thraxian.

Then he heard a noise.

Whoosh.

Something wrapped around his sword arm.

He yanked against it, and saw that one of the Thraxians had fired some sort of weapon. The metallic rope was wrapped around his arm, connecting him back to the large crossbow the Thraxian held.

Galen pulled hard and the Thraxian stumbled. Then, he righted himself and fired again.

A second rope shot out, wrapping around Galen's other arm.

Drak. He tried to maneuver his sword up to cut the metal ropes.

Whoosh. A third rope wrapped around his middle. He fought against it, but he noticed the ropes were starting to glow.

The ropes tightened around his body, pressing his arms to his sides, and they were now a brilliant gold. They began to burn wherever they touched his bare skin.

"Cowards," he roared.

The Thraxians advanced. "We do what is necessary for the might of the House of Thrax."

"There is no House of Thrax anymore," Galen said.

One Thraxian raised his sword, pressing the tip to Galen's gut. "Now you die, and there will be no House of Galen."

A body flew at the alien.

Sam landed on the Thraxian's head, neatly avoiding his horns. With a twist of her thighs, she took the alien down. Galen heard the Thraxian's neck snap.

Galen dropped down and kicked out with his leg, knocking over another Thraxian.

When Sam rose, she stood between Galen and the others. *Protecting him.*

"Sam, move!"

She ignored him. "Release the ropes. Now."

No one moved.

Shouts echoed across the arena. Galen's gladiators poured onto the sand from a tunnel on the opposite side. They raced across the arena floor, followed by several House of Rone cyborgs.

"For honor and freedom," Raiden roared.

The gladiators echoed his cry.

The Thraxian holding the rope weapon dropped it. The other aliens that were still standing stepped back toward the ship, all of them watching the incoming gladiators.

Sam grabbed the closest rope, pulling on it. "Galen."

"Careful it doesn't burn you."

"Hold on and I'll get you free." She yanked the weapon across the sand.

Then he saw one of the Thraxians appear right behind her. "Sam!"

She spun, but she wasn't fast enough. The Thraxian swung his sword.

Sam tried to dodge, but the tip of the sword flashed across her throat. Blood sprayed.

"No!" Galen roared.

Sam's eyes widened and her body went limp. She started to fall.

Heart pounding, Galen used all his strength against the ropes still holding him. He felt his veins bulging and his muscles straining. His tattoos flashed.

The ropes burst apart.

He saw the Thraxian running back toward the ship,

but he didn't watch. He dropped down beside Sam, gathering her into his arms. He reached over his shoulder and ripped his cloak off. *Drak*, there was blood everywhere. He pressed the fabric against her neck.

"Hold on, Sam," he ordered.

Her gaze locked with his. Her eyes were filled with pain.

The Thraxian ship took off, bathing them in a gust of heat.

"Stay with me." Galen stroked her cheek. "You are the strongest person I've ever met. Stay with me."

Raiden and the others reached them.

"Medical," Galen yelled. "Now!"

CHAPTER TEN

Galen paced Medical as his healers worked on Sam.

When they lowered her limp body into one of the regen tanks, he still couldn't shake the emotions storming through him. In his head, he just kept seeing that sword slicing across her throat, the blood. So much blood.

His healers kept shooting him nervous glances. He was well aware they weren't used to seeing him so worked up, and his tattoos were still glowing.

"Galen." Raiden stepped up beside him. "She's going to be okay?"

"That's what they tell me."

"She's tough. You've always said the women from Earth are tough to the bone, but Sam has tough running through her veins."

A little bit of the knot in Galen's chest eased. Sam's face looked relaxed as she floated in the blue gel in the tank. Still, he wouldn't be satisfied until she opened her brown eyes and talked to him.

"Your tattoos haven't glowed since I was a teenager," Raiden said.

Galen turned his head. "Since you were old enough to defend yourself."

"Royal guards were given an extract from a plant on Aurelia. It was dangerous, but if a guard survived, it enhanced their strength in battle."

"The *shidlea* plant." Galen remembered how bad the extract had tasted and how sick it had made him. It had been an honor to be given it.

"It activated when a person the guard cared about, their charge or their mate, was in danger," Raiden murmured.

Galen remained silent.

Then Raiden grinned. "Drak, G, you're falling for her. You, a man who vowed to never love a woman. You, a man who rolled his eyes at all of us who fell for these Earth women."

"Enjoying yourself?" Galen asked.

"Oh, I'm barely getting started and just wait until the others find out."

Galen was fucked, to borrow an Earth phrase. He looked at Sam again and couldn't bring himself to be that concerned about it.

"I couldn't have designed a better woman for you," Raiden said. "Sam Santos is strength personified, but she's not hard. She has a...softness isn't the right word, a suppleness. You know she can fight but cares as well."

"I don't deserve her."

Raiden hissed out a breath. "You deserve her and so much more, Galen. You have done nothing but protect me, and then the people of your House, not to mention all the captives you've helped rescue from the arena. You give, you stand as a shield, and you never ask for anything in return." He looked at the tank. "I think that maybe she's your reward. Don't screw it up."

"I already did. I pushed her away last night. I hurt her." Galen's hand curled into a fist. "She nearly died today."

"Another mark against the *drakking* Thraxians, not you. And if you screwed up with her, that just makes you mortal like the rest of us. You make it up to her and make her realize how important she is."

Galen kept his gaze on Sam.

"It's time we stop the Thraxians and their ugly plans," Raiden said.

Galen nodded. "I need to reschedule my meet with Mortas." The self-important imperator would treat the delay as an insult.

"I'll take care of it." Raiden gripped his shoulder. "You stay with her."

"Thanks, Raiden."

"And brace yourself."

Galen turned his head. "For what?"

"For the ribbing, teasing, and general taunting your friends are going to throw your way."

Galen managed a smile. "As long as she wakes up, I don't care."

With another slap on Galen's back, Raiden left. Galen dragged a chair over to Sam's regen tank.

Winter appeared. "Galen, she's going to be fine, but she won't wake up for a few hours. Why don't you—"

"I'm staying."

Winter bit her lip. "I'll call you when—"

"I'm not leaving, Winter."

She huffed out a breath. "Oh, fine. Don't think that I can't see what's going on here."

He raised a brow.

With a smile, Winter leaned closer. "And don't think for a second that I'm not sharing all the juicy details with the others." She reached over and touched his cheek before moving away.

Galen leaned forward, resting his elbows on his knees, and kept his gaze locked on Sam.

SHE WAS FLOATING and it felt good. Sam felt like she was swimming at her favorite beach close to her *abuela's* house in Puerto Rico.

Then she frowned. This wasn't the beach. Something felt...off. Lights. Quiet murmurs. Sharp, clean scents. All around her body she felt a sticky, cool goo. Slowly, she cracked open her eyes.

"Hey there, Sam. You're okay. You're in a regen tank here in Medical."

Sam turned her head slightly, and saw Winter's pretty face with her one blue eye and one milky white eye.

"What happened?" Sam tried to sort through her foggy memories.

"You were injured in a fight with the Thraxians."

Just that one word brought all the memories back. She sat up, gripping the edge of the tank. "Galen—"

"Is fine." Winter pressed a finger to her lips and tilted her head.

Sam spotted Galen, asleep in a chair beside her regen tank.

"He refused to leave your side," Winter said quietly. "Even after I assured him you were going to be okay. He just fell asleep."

So many feelings were working and tumbling through Sam. She saw that while he'd cleaned up a bit, there were still dried streaks of blood on his face.

"Oh, your injury is all healed, too, if you're interested." Winter sounded amused.

"I'm all clear?"

"Yes. Perfectly healthy."

Winter helped Sam out of the tank, helped her clean off the last of the blue healing gel sticking to her skin, and handed her a silver-gray robe. She wrapped it around herself, and then knelt by Galen's chair.

His eye opened and his gaze sharpened on her. "You're all right." His voice was gritty from sleep.

She nodded resting her hand on his thigh. He leaned down, cupping her chin.

His fingers moved lower, caressing her neck. She remembered the sting and shock of the wound. The warm mist of blood.

Suddenly, Galen stood, and a second later, he scooped her up into his arms.

Oh. Apart from being carted around by her captors,

usually with her fighting them every step of the way, she'd never been carried so carefully before. Like she was something precious.

She felt everyone in Medical staring at them, but they both ignored the looks.

Galen strode out and down the corridor. They moved past where his high-level gladiators had their quarters, and down the long hall leading to his suite. He nodded at the guards as they opened the door. He headed through his living area and up the stairs Sam had seen before.

She looked around the room with interest. "Your inner sanctum."

He stopped in the middle of the large space. It was three times the size of her bedroom. There was an enormous bed resting on a platform at the far end of the room, covered in a sleek black cover. Above it was an amazing skylight that let light filter in. At the head of the bed, a striking painting graced the wall. It showed a lone gladiator wearing a beaten metal helmet, topped with a red plume, in an empty arena. His sword pointed to the ground and his head was bowed. She knew instantly that the strong body in the image belonged to Galen.

Everything else in the room was neat and tidy. Exactly as she expected of him.

He strode over and set her on the bed. "I'll order you some food."

She nodded, watching as he went back downstairs. She heard his deep voice as he spoke with somebody.

When he came back, he started to pace the room, not speaking. She could tell he was tense. There was a knock on the door below, and Galen disappeared and returned carrying a tray over to her.

"Here." He set the tray down beside her.

Sam looked at the offerings—berries, freshly-made bread, cheese-like cubes.

She pulled in a breath. More of the foods she'd told him she'd craved. When she looked up, he was staring at her.

"I'm okay, Galen."

"And I'll believe it...eventually."

She set the tray on the bedside table and reached up. She loosened the neck of her robe. "See. Healed."

He moved closer and reached out. He stroked a long finger over her neck, then along her collarbone.

Her eyelids fluttered and she trembled. His touch felt so good, and she felt the pulse of it between her legs. "Galen."

He pulled away. "You need to rest." He stalked to the windows, staring outside, his back tense.

Noble to the core, this man. It was as admirable as it was annoying.

"I just got out of a regen tank. I feel wonderful." She rose and walked to him. "I need you to give me what I need."

He spun to face her. "And what's that?"

Sam shrugged out of the robe. It slithered to the floor.

She stood there, naked, and felt the heat of his gaze burn through her. His gaze moved downward, like he was drinking her all in, before it slowly moved back to her face.

"I need you," she said. "Your lips, your hands, your tongue, your cock."

"Sam." A tortured groan.

"I had everything taken from me. And had so much horror forced on me." She stood proud before him. "Now I'm choosing what *I* want."

She watched Galen's battle-scarred hands curl into fists. She could see him fighting some internal battle.

Then he closed the space between them in one short stride. He gripped her shoulders. "I'll give you what you want." His fingers dug into her skin. "But be warned, I'll take everything, Samantha. I want it *all*."

Her breath hitched. "Show me, boss-man."

SHE WAS GORGEOUS.

Galen stroked his hands down Sam's sides. So strong and all woman. He skimmed a hand over her hip and then down one thigh. She reminded him of the warrior goddesses of Aurelia, and some primal part of him wanted to fall on his knees and worship her.

He stroked his hand back up her leg, hearing her indrawn breath. He nudged her legs apart and dropped to his knees. He pressed a kiss to her taut belly, eyeing the patch of dark curls at the juncture of her thighs.

"Galen—"

"I want to see you, Sam." He looked up her body, vowing to give those rounded breasts some attention later. "I want to give you pleasure."

She licked her lips, her dark eyes on him. She nodded.

Galen moved his fingers through her dark curls, then stroked deeper. His fingers moved through her soft, warm folds.

Her hands clamped on his shoulders. He took his time, caressing her and learning what she liked. He was a patient man, and he planned to use every bit of it to learn how to drive her crazy.

Her hips jerked on his hand and he slid one finger inside her. She moaned. *Drak*, it wasn't enough. He slid another finger inside, where she was tight and warm.

No, not enough. He pulled his fingers out, wrapped his arms around her, and pushed to his feet, lifting her up.

She gave a small cry and he crossed the room, laying her back on his bed.

"Open your legs, Sam."

She looked at him, her hair spilling around her face. There was heat and hunger in her gaze. This wasn't a woman who submitted easily.

Anything she gave freely would be a gift.

She let her legs fall open. Open to him.

Galen felt desire claw his insides. He pressed one knee to the bed, kneeling between her legs, gazing at her pink folds. It had been so long since he'd allowed himself pleasure, and he was planning to gorge himself on this woman.

"So *drakking* pretty." He stroked her again, watching pleasure cross her face. Then he found that small nub that all his *drakking* gladiators had been so obsessed with since the Earth women had crashed into their lives. He rolled her swollen clitoris between his fingers.

Her hips jerked up, her hands clenching in the covers.

Galen lowered his head, breathing in the musky scent of her. Then he licked her.

"Galen... *Dios*." She moaned, long and loud.

He sucked and licked her, lapping at her and stabbing his tongue inside her. He loved the taste of her. *More*. He needed more.

Her hands curled into his hair. "I want to touch you."

"This is about your pleasure."

She pulled on his hair hard, until he looked up her gorgeous body and met her gaze.

"You're allowed pleasure too, Galen." She stroked his cheek. "This is about *our* pleasure."

No one had concerned themselves with his pleasure...ever. He'd never let anyone close enough.

Sam reared up, her hands moving to his chest and pushing his shirt up and off. Then she leaned forward and put her lips on him. He groaned. Her tongue moved over his nipples, her teeth nipping at his muscles.

"I love your body," she murmured. "So hard and tough. Strong."

Her tongue traced over his scars and Galen jerked. Then her teeth sank into his shoulder. He hoped it was hard enough to leave a mark. Then her tongue danced over his skin, and he realized she was tracing his tattoos.

"I saw these glow," she murmured.

Desire was like a fire in his blood. He felt his control crumbling. Control he never gave up. Ever. "Yes."

"What's that mean?"

"It signifies an increase in my strength, when I need to protect someone I care about."

She laved the ink again with her tongue. Her hands moved over his stomach, trailing over the ridges there. Then she moved down, cupping his hard cock through his leathers.

Galen growled. *Enough.* He pushed her back on the bed. He pressed a hand to her belly, holding her there as he put his mouth between her legs again.

"*Oh.* Galen." Her hands twisted in his hair again. "Yes. More."

He sucked harder. She was so damn addictive, and he'd never get enough of the taste of her. Her hips lifted up again and he groaned against her. With another suck, she cried out, arching as she screamed his name.

Body shaking, Galen stood. He tore his trousers open, his skin feeling too tight for his body. He shed the rest of his clothes methodically.

Sam rose up on one elbow, watching him. She was panting, her breasts jiggling with each shift of her chest. Then he reached down and circled one ankle. He dragged her closer to the edge of the bed.

Galen knelt on the bed, hitching her leg over his arm and opening her to him. With his other hand, he reached down and stroked his swollen cock.

Her gaze dropped, hungry. "Yes."

He covered her, notching his cock against her.

"Now," she cried. "Please."

He thrust inside her.

Drak. Drak. Their mingled groans were loud. She

writhed against him and he started to move.

He pounded inside her. He knew there was no finesse and no rhythm. This wasn't an elegant loving. This was mating—pure and simple.

"You feel that?" He ground himself inside her.

"Yes," she breathed. "*Dios*, you fill me up."

Need made his chest tight. "Who's inside you?"

"You are."

"Say my name."

"Galen." Her eyes met his. "Galen, you're inside me."

He gritted his teeth against the wave of pleasure. She was so tight and hot.

Her eyes fluttered closed.

"No, Sam. Eyes on me," he growled.

She opened them again.

"Good. I want to watch when you come."

The sound of skin slapping against skin filled the room. All Galen could feel was the need riding him hard, and her body clenched tight around his cock.

He shifted the angle of his thrusts, grinding against her clit.

She cried out. "Galen, I'm going to…"

"Let go, Sam. Give yourself to me. I've got you."

She cried out, her head thrashing against the covers. Pleasure spasmed across her face, and he felt the rhythmic pulses of her body clamping down on him.

With two more wild thrusts, Galen lodged his cock deep inside her. He leaned over her, setting his teeth into the spot where her shoulder met her neck. He bit down, hearing her cry out again. His orgasm ripped through him, the fierce pleasure tearing him apart.

CHAPTER ELEVEN

G alen's sexy growl shivered through Sam.

She looked up, her breath catching. She could look at him all day, especially like this.

He had his back to the headboard of the big bed, his legs bent and cocked, as she knelt between his powerful thighs. His hands were tangled in her hair and his cock was in her mouth.

Sam sucked him deeper. *Dios*, she loved the feel of him, so hard but silky. And the salty, musky taste of him.

He was spread out for her, all muscled strength and those amazing tattoos. He growled again, his hips thrusting upward. Oh yeah, she loved this. As his fingers clenched in her hair, Sam felt potent and in control.

She could bring this powerful, controlled man to the edge. She sucked harder, bobbing up and down on him. Her own desire was strumming through her and she knew she was wetter than she'd ever been.

"Enough." His powerful arms jerked her up and before she was ready, she was straddling him, her face inches from his.

His cock slammed inside her.

She moaned, her head dropping back.

"Eyes to me, Sam."

She'd learned over their hours in his bed that he liked to watch her. He liked to watch what he did to her and watch her come apart.

As she met that icy gaze that was now so familiar to her, she saw the glittering heat in the cool blue.

He moved his head, his mouth brushing over her shoulder. She felt him kiss the mark he'd left on her neck. His mark. A claiming.

"I've never had anything that was just mine," he said.

Her heart clenched. "Galen—"

"I was raised to serve, not to have." His hands clamped on her hips, driving her up and down on his cock. "I've never had something that was just for me."

"I'm right here, Galen."

"Even my House...it was always for Raiden, then for the others who joined it."

Sam felt a pull toward him that was so powerful. "I'm yours. Just for you."

A loud sound tore from his chest. He reared up and his cock slid out of her. Before she could do more than gasp, he flipped her, and she found her belly pressed to the bed.

Behind her, she felt him grip her thigh and then he thrust back in.

Dios. The hot shock of it made her moan, and she turned to press her cheek to the sheets.

His hands moved to grip hers, his big body covering hers. He pulled her arms above her head, his fingers tangling with hers as he pounded her into the bed.

"You're mine now." His voice was deep and rough. "Not just House of Galen, *mine.*"

She thrust back against him. "Yes."

He plunged deeper, until she couldn't tell where he ended and she began.

"You aren't alone anymore, Sam. Never again."

His breath was hot on her neck, his cock stretching her, and ripples spread through her body.

"I'll be your shield, your protector, your champion. Wherever you need me, I'll stand beside you, behind you, or kneel at your feet. Whatever you need."

His words sent her higher and she cried out. She felt one hand slip down her back, sliding over her skin, worshiping her. She arched into his touch and his hand moved beneath her. A second later, he circled her clit and a cry tore from her.

Her orgasm hit, huge and frightening, stealing her breath away. Pleasure shuddered through her and she pushed back against him mindlessly.

A harsh sound came from Galen. He slammed into her one more time and pressed his face to her neck. As he came, he sank his teeth into that same sensitive spot where he'd already marked her.

The possessive gesture drove her up again and she cried out his name.

GALEN LANDED ON THE BED, pulling Sam close to his side. He pressed his face against her neck.

He traced lazy circles on her skin. All that beautiful, golden skin that he couldn't get enough of. He felt where he'd bitten her, a possessive mark he liked seeing on her.

What they'd done here in his bed...it had pulled him apart and put him back together.

"That was..." Her voice was husky and soft.

He looked down at her. She looked tired, satisfied, and a little smug.

"I don't have words." Her cheeks were flushed and there was a smile on her lips.

"I know," he said.

She leaned over and pressed a kiss to his chest. "You're just too damn sexy, Imperator Galen."

His gut clenched. No one had ever called him sexy before. He was nothing compared to her. She was so beautiful, still so feminine, when he was hard and scarred. But she was looking at him like she wanted him inside her again.

"Next time I'm inside you," he said. "And you're clenching on me so hard as you come, you can call me imperator."

She laughed, elbowing him. Then she reached up and touched his eye patch. "You ever take this off?"

He shook his head. "It's not pretty. Just scars."

Her hand drifted down to his chest, stroking the nasty scars there as well. Marks he'd never had medically fixed or removed.

"You got them escaping Aurelia," she said quietly.

"Yes." A ripple of tension moved through him. Old pain twisted up like a desert serpent ready to strike.

"Will you tell me?" she murmured.

"It's an ugly story." And it wasn't one he'd shared with anybody. He and Raiden had discussed certain aspects of their history and their escape from their homeworld, but they were men, they didn't linger over it.

Strangely, he found himself wanting to talk to Sam. *Drak*, why did he feel like she cracked him wide open?

"I did what I had to in order to save Raiden. Thraxian mercenaries had us cornered, and I was injured getting us free. I have no regrets about that." Only that Raiden had already witnessed the slaying of his family, and Galen hadn't been able to save them, or stop the destruction of their homeworld.

"Brave, heroic man," Sam murmured.

"I was doing my job."

"I don't think Raiden was ever just a job to you."

Galen pulled her closer, breathing in the scent of her hair.

"You did right by him, Galen." She leaned up to kiss his eye patch, then moved to press her lips to the scars on his chest. "You are a hero."

He sat up. "I've done a lot of things to ensure Raiden's safety and build this House. Not all of them were heroic. A world like Carthago breeds survivors, not heroes."

"The women have told me all about the work you do here, behind the scenes. Rescuing captives unsuited to the arena from the other houses." She brushed her thumb across his lips. "You think I'm not going to respect you for doing what needs to be done? You think I don't understand what it is to do what you have to do to live, even when it destroys little pieces of your soul?"

He slid his hand into her hair. "Sam—"

"I understand. And I think what you achieved here, what you forged from nothing, is amazing."

He did the only thing he could and kissed her.

When she pulled back, she was breathless. She groaned. "I have to go. I promised to meet Harper, Rory, and the others."

Galen nodded, but he was reluctant to let her loose. To lose their private time together. "And I have to meet with the imperators."

Her face turned serious. "You'll find me when you get back? Tell me how it went?"

He nodded again, tracing her healed neck once more.

She smiled. "I think I just proved beyond a doubt that I'm okay."

"I'm not sure I'm entirely convinced."

She climbed off the bed, seemingly unconcerned that she was naked. He greedily drank in all those glorious curves.

"Guess I'll have to prove it to you again later." She shot him a saucy wink as she headed for the bathroom.

Galen wanted to grab her and drag her back into his bed. His cock was already hardening just from looking at her. He'd lost track of how many times he'd already had her, but his body didn't care. He wanted her like he'd never wanted anything before.

Sam Santos would never, ever suffer again. He made the vow to himself. He'd make sure of it.

As for keeping her... He looked at the tangled sheets of his bed. She'd just escaped hell. She needed space to decide what she wanted, and whether that included a man loaded with responsibilities and with a past of failure.

He wouldn't push, and if she decided that she didn't want him, he'd find a way to live with that.

After Sam left to meet her friends, Galen dressed and headed to his office. He had a meeting to prepare for.

What he hadn't expected was to find his office crowded with his gladiators. He pulled up short in the doorway.

Raiden was standing at the window with Blaine and Saff, while Thorin leaned against the wall. Kace and Nero were standing by the door, and Lore was happily sitting in Galen's chair like it was his office.

Lore spotted him first. "So." The gladiator drawled the word, a huge grin on his face.

Galen should have expected this. He strode inside.

"How the mighty have fallen." Raiden made no attempt to hide his smile.

"I'm just happy he finally got laid," Thorin said. "It has been a *long* time."

Galen scowled at all of them.

"How's it feel?" Saff asked. "To fall under the spell of an Earth woman?"

"Out of my chair," Galen growled at Lore.

The long-haired gladiator stood, waving to the chair

with a flourish. Then his face turned serious. "We're happy for you, G."

Galen sat. "She is..." He had no idea how to describe Sam and what she made him feel.

Kace nodded. "We know. They worm their way under your skin, and leave you frustrated and dazzled at the same time."

"And nothing has ever felt so right," Nero finished.

Blaine pressed a hand to Galen's desk. "Sam is one of the best people I know. She's also my friend... You hurt her—" The man from Earth left the rest of his sentence unspoken, but Galen knew exactly what Blaine meant.

"Noted, gladiator."

Thorin shook his head. "Never thought I'd see Galen fall for a woman. It looks pretty good on you, G."

Galen fought back a smile. "If you're all finished rubbing it in, I have a meeting to attend."

Instantly, the atmosphere in his office changed.

Raiden walked forward. "Your meeting with the imperators."

Galen nodded. "I need to bring them together." Images of Sam's blood spraying across the arena sand filled his head. "I need them to understand the threat the Thraxians and their implants pose. I need all their fighters to come together."

"You don't think they'll agree, after what you have to tell them?" Blaine asked.

"The imperators have a long history of minding their own business." Galen frowned. "I'm asking them to fight, to spill blood, and to end another House, once and for all."

"There's no telling what they'll decide," Raiden said.

Galen stood. "I'll do what I can, and we have to hope we get enough allies together so we can end the Thraxians."

"And stop them before it's too late," Blaine added.

CHAPTER TWELVE

S am lifted the drink that Regan had made her and took a sip. It didn't taste too bad. If she didn't think about it too closely, the beverage tasted almost like coffee.

Around her, the women were talking and laughing. She felt something brush her ankle, and looked down at the robot dog, Hero, sniffing at her feet. She smiled. The dog abandoned her a moment later to go back over to baby Finley, who was playing on a blanket on the living room floor. The baby grinned and clapped his hands. The two were best friends.

Cute.

"Sooooo, Sam got naked with our hunk-a-licious imperator."

Rory's words almost made Sam spray her drink every-where. She looked up and saw that everyone was watching her. "Excuse me?"

"He didn't leave her side in Medical," Winter added.

"And when she was healed, he scooped her right up and carried her off." The doctor sighed.

"Hey, isn't that breaking patient confidentiality or something?" Sam complained.

Winter smiled. "We aren't on Earth anymore."

"And there are no secrets around here," Madeline added.

Rory grinned widely. "Besides, you have a rather large bruise there on your neck. Doesn't look like a training injury."

"Looks like a possessive alpha male mark to me," Mia said with a smile.

Sam automatically fingered the mark, remembering exactly how she'd gotten it. She fought off a shiver. A part of her never wanted it to fade.

"Come on," Rory leaned back in her chair. "We all have our own alien gladiator hunks, but if you think that we all haven't wondered about that hard-bodied man, you're crazy."

Harper, sitting next to Sam on the couch, rolled her eyes. "Ignore her." Harper scooped Finley off the floor and started bouncing him on her knee.

"No, don't," Mia said. "I've wondered." The small woman got a faraway look in her eye. "He's always so...controlled."

Madeline crossed her legs. "I want to know too. I've wondered what happens when a man like Galen loses all that control."

Sam blinked, her throat tightening. She'd missed this. She missed having friends who cared, and poked and prodded.

She set her drink down on the table. "It's good."

"Good." Rory looked insulted. "That's it?"

"Really good." Sam thought of touching Galen, his big body moving over hers. "It's beyond anything you can imagine." She still felt a sweet ache between her legs.

The women giggled, and Rory fell back in her chair. "I think I just had a mini orgasm."

"Rory." Harper covered Finley's ears. The baby chuckled.

"He's a super alien baby, but he has no idea what I'm talking about yet." Rory grabbed her son, nuzzling him.

"Things are kind of intense," Sam said. "For now, I'm focused on taking down the Thraxians."

"And getting as much hot sex as you can." Rory winked and then looked down at her son. "Don't listen to mama, baby boy."

There was more laughter.

A House of Galen worker entered the room with a swish of skirts. "Mistress Samantha, the imperator has returned, and asks that you join him."

"I bet," Rory said.

But Sam felt tension creep in. She exchanged a glance with Harper and stood. "Regan, I liked the *rica*. Thanks. I'll see you all later."

She headed out and turned in the direction of Galen's office. When she reached the doorway, she saw him at his desk, elbows resting on the surface. There was a dark and heavy vibe filling the room.

"Galen?"

He looked up, and one look at his face made her stomach drop. "It didn't go well."

"It didn't go well." A muscle ticked in his jaw. "I have my allies, like the House of Rone and the House of Zeringei, and a few others. But in order to guarantee success, I need all the houses to get on board with this fight."

She moved closer. "They don't see the implant as a big problem?"

"Like I've told you, there's a long history of the houses minding their own business. And some are arrogant enough to believe the Thraxians aren't a threat."

Sam dropped into the chair across from his desk. "That's why you've rescued prisoners under the radar."

He nodded. "It was easier than causing outright conflict with the other houses. Some of the other imperators are just arrogant fools, and others believe they are too powerful. The rest just don't want to believe."

"So where does that leave us?"

His head snapped up, his face determined. "We fight. I got word from Zhim when I returned that Zaabha has landed."

Sam's chest locked. "Where?"

"In the Forsaken Barrens, north of the city. It hasn't moved for several hours."

Blood roared in her ears. "It's a trap."

"Yes, but I don't give a *drak*, Sam. I'll pull my people and my allies together. Rillian has promised soldiers as well. We'll likely still be outnumbered, and we'll be in their terrain, but nothing will stop us. We'll go in and destroy the implant research, we rescue the prisoners, and then burn Zaabha to the ground."

She knew this was going to be beyond dangerous. She

was well aware that Galen had some of the best fighters on the planet, but the Thraxians had numbers. They had prisoners, and fighters with implants that made them willing to follow every order.

To kill without hesitation.

Sam pressed her hands to her thighs, her nails digging through her trousers. There was a part of her that didn't want to see the Zaabha Arena again, but she couldn't let that part take over. All her life, she'd always stood up for what she believed in.

Galen pulled in a deep breath. "I've learned a lot about teamwork and determination from having stubborn, resilient humans under my roof. I've learned that the odds don't always predict who'll win the day."

She smiled, but she knew it didn't reach her eyes.

He sat back in his chair, like a king on his throne. "I don't want you on the mission."

Sam's stomach revolted. She watched his hands curl into fists on the desktop.

"But I know you want to go," he said, before she could protest. "I know you'll need to go, and that you deserve to be a part of ending this."

Her chest loosened. "Thank you."

"I also know that you're strong enough to bring the Thraxians to their knees. It will be my honor to fight beside you."

Dios, he gutted her. Sam stood and circled the desk. She'd never in all her life met a man like Galen. A man of conviction, one who was a pillar of self-confidence, and wasn't afraid to show how much he respected her.

She cupped Galen's rugged face and leaned down to kiss him.

Instantly, his mouth moved against hers, deepening the kiss. He yanked her into his lap. She slid her hands into his hair, her tongue tangling with his.

"Now," he said. "I need you now." His hands went to her trousers, flicking them open.

"Someone might come in."

He pushed her trousers down, and she lifted her hips to help him.

"I don't care."

A second later, her trousers were gone, and he opened his own. Sam didn't care, either. Desire ignited like fire in her blood. She straddled him and then he thrust inside her.

There. She moaned. So good.

Sam lifted her hips and started riding him. Their gazes locked, their lips just a whisper apart.

"You will not get hurt," he said with a growl.

"You aren't allowed to get hurt, either."

His hands clenched on her hips driving her up and down. "You are so *drakking* beautiful, Sam."

She moved faster, and soon, there were no thoughts of anything—only the connection between them and the pleasure crashing over them.

GALEN STRODE INTO VARUS' stables, Sam and his gladiators beside him. It was early, and a hush still lay over Kor Magna.

"Galen." The big man strode forward to meet them, his face serious. The former gladiator was huge, with a grizzled face and a shaved head.

"Varus," Galen greeted him.

A young girl trotted beside Varus. The teen, Duna, was one of Varus' best desert guides.

"I hear you're going to war," Varus said.

Galen gave a nod. "As I said in my message, we need *tarnids*. Zaabha is in the Forsaken Barrens."

"Horrible place." Duna's nose wrinkled.

"Zaabha is a *drakking* abomination," Varus spat. "The Thraxians and their sand-sucking allies the Srinar, as well." He turned to Duna. "Have the team bring the beasts."

"I'll have payment delivered to you," Galen said.

The man shook his head. "No. Consider this my contribution to the fight."

Galen nodded, clasping hands with the former gladiator in a warrior's hold. "Thank you."

Galen saw Varus' gaze shift past him, and knew the man was looking at Sam. Galen couldn't stop himself reaching for her and sliding an arm around her waist.

He'd made love to her that morning—hard and rough. They'd torn up the sheets, desperate for each other. But despite gorging himself on her, he felt desire spike.

Varus studied her, his bushy eyebrows rising. "So, you're Galen's latest rescue."

"Actually, she rescued me," Galen said.

"We rescued each other," Sam said.

Galen smiled. "Sam, this is Varus. Varus, Sam Santos."

"Hello." She held out a hand and Varus shook it.

"You have a good grip." He studied her. "I can tell you're a fighter. And if you're half as tenacious as the other Earth women, you're a good match for the best man I know."

Sam's lips twitched. "Thank you."

Varus looked at Galen. "You're letting her fight?"

Galen smiled wryly. "You probably shouldn't have said that."

"He doesn't *let* me do anything," Sam said. "Besides, this is my fight too."

"Sam was the Champion of Zaabha, Varus."

The big man's eyes went wide. "Then not just a fighter, and even more tenacious than all those Earth women put together. Good luck to you both."

"We'll take it," Galen said.

"I can lead you into the Forsaken Barrens," Duna said, chin jutting.

Galen shook his head. "We know where we're going, but thank you." He didn't want the young girl anywhere near Zaabha.

She looked like she was going to complain, but Varus gripped her slim shoulder and squeezed.

It wasn't long before they were riding out into the desert. Galen was at the lead, riding one of the six-legged *tarnids*. Sam rode beside him, and his gladiators were close behind. Rillian's soldiers were flying in on his ship once Galen's team arrived at Zaabha.

Nearby, House of Rone and House of Zeringei gladiators, as well as Vek, were jogging in perfect rhythm. The *tarnids* didn't particularly like the cyborgs, or the beast-like Zeringei and Vek riding them.

Galen's gaze was drawn back to Sam. She looked like a warrior queen, seated like she'd ridden a *tarnid* a hundred times before.

She was going back to the place of her nightmares. Her prison. He so desperately wanted to protect her from it.

Whatever happened, Galen would ensure her safety and survival.

Raiden came up beside him on a *tarnid* with dark-green scales. His beast nudged Galen's.

"Are you ready to fight?" Galen asked.

"Yes." Raiden's eyes flashed. "I'm more than ready."

"Raiden, whatever happens, you protect Sam."

His friend, the man who was his family, looked at him. "You know I will."

"Raiden—" Galen couldn't find the words he wanted to say. This man was his closest friend, his family, his charge, his son.

Raiden reached out and clasped Galen's arm. "I know."

The hours passed, the suns beating down on them. Sweat trickled in a continuous slide down Galen's back, but he ignored it.

Suddenly, Sam called out. "Galen!"

She pointed ahead, and he followed her gaze. In the distance, the imposing shape of Zaabha sat, unmoving, resting on the sand.

Galen scowled. The hellhole crouched on the sand like some ugly, evil beast.

Resolve filled him. The Thraxians had hurt too many people and destroyed too many lives. It wasn't just the humans who'd had their lives shattered. There were far too many to count.

Today, that ended.

CHAPTER THIRTEEN

I t was eerie stepping back into the arena. Walking willingly back into her own personal hell and torture chamber.

Sam looked around the place where she had fought to hold on to herself.

It was empty. Silent. The stands were bare, and below, the cell doors stood open. Abandoned.

"What the *drak*?" Thorin's deep voice.

"There's no one here." Raiden stood with his hands on his hips, frowning.

Beside Sam, Galen turned in a slow circle, his face considering. "They're here, somewhere."

"They lured us here for a reason," Sam said.

"We need to check the labs." Galen nodded at Magnus.

The cyborg moved toward a doorway heading down into the tunnels and his cyborgs followed, breaking into a jog.

"They won't find anything." Sam's heart was a steady beat in her ears.

"We'll find them." Galen looked at her. "Where do you think they went?"

She shook her head. She didn't know.

Galen lifted a small, metallic communicator. "Zhim? Are you picking us up?"

Scratchy static came through. Then Zhim's voice. "Connection...not good."

"I need you and Ryan to search the system. Zaabha is empty. The Thraxians must have a base or something nearby."

"Will...see what..."

"Say again?"

"Scientist...signal strong. Need to..."

Suddenly, the ground started to vibrate. Galen cursed.

"What the hell?" Harper called out, lifting both her swords. From just behind her, Vek growled.

The gladiators all pulled in closer. Raiden moved in behind Harper. Saff and Blaine moved to stand back to back. Nero and Lore spread their feet, weapons raised. Everyone fought to keep their balance.

Ahead, Sam watched as rectangular holes opened up in the arena floor, sand pouring through.

"Run!" Galen barked.

Sam sprinted forward, breaking away toward the stands. But as she watched, the stands in front of her started to tilt and topple over.

Just a few meters away, Harper leaped over a hole.

With a flap of his red cloak, Raiden jumped right behind her.

Galen moved up beside Sam, grabbing her hand. A hole opened in front of them and together, they leaped over it.

But instantly, another cavity opened up directly below Sam. Her foot hit open space.

Shit. She yanked her hand from Galen's. She tried to grab onto the edge of the hole, but her hand slipped on the sand. She tumbled into the blackness.

"Sam!" Galen shouted.

Below, all she could see was darkness.

She heard shouts and the sound of others falling. Sand streamed past her.

Before she knew it, she hit the ground, pain jarring through her body. Trying to catch her breath, she pressed her face to the rocky ground. Nearby, she heard other bodies smacking into the ground. She groaned, pushing up on her hands and knees.

She looked up, and for a fleeting second, she thought she saw jagged, rock walls, with burning torches attached to them.

Then she blinked and felt a burst of pain in her head.

Everything went black, and when she opened her eyes, everything inside her went still.

Beneath her were cool sheets and a soft bunk. She was in her bed on Fortuna Station. Confusion swept through her. She blinked again. It wasn't right, she was... She was somewhere else just before, doing...something.

Her head hurt and she reached up to rub her temple.

She had the overwhelming sensation that she was forgetting something. Something important.

"Captain Santos, you have five minutes until your duty shift starts," the comp beside her bed intoned.

With a curse, she slid out of bed, reaching for her clothes. Everything in her quarters was as it always was—fairly neat and tidy except for yesterday's clothes tossed over a chair. She pulled on her uniform, fingering the Fortuna Station logo stitched on her chest, and wondered why it felt wrong.

Feeling uneasy, she touched the door control and headed into the corridor. A large bank of long windows gave a fantastic view of Jupiter below.

The click of boots. She turned and saw Blaine striding toward her. Her head throbbed painfully again.

"Hey, Captain." He fell into step beside her. "I wanted to go over tomorrow's roster with you."

"Sure. Blaine, did anything unusual happen last night?"

The big man frowned. "No. Everything was normal. Why?"

She shook her head. "I keep feeling like I'm forgetting something."

"Only thing different is that I've had a headache from hell this morning," he said.

She paused, discomfited. "Me too."

All of a sudden, there was a flash of light through the windows. Sam looked up and watched a small ship whizz past the station. Then another. And another.

"*Madre de Dios?*" she whispered.

Sirens began to wail, and the wall beside them started

to glow a deep orange. She and Blaine both whipped up their laser weapons. A second later, the wall collapsed inward, and a being like something out of a nightmare stepped through.

Alien. A demon-like alien that was huge, with cracked, dark skin and orange veins glowing beneath, a set of horns, and glowing eyes.

Suddenly, Sam heard screams echoing through the station. Blaine started shouting.

Sam just stared, horror and fear flooding her.

Thraxians.

Thraxians? Why did she know that name?

She saw Blaine stride forward, firing his weapon and engaging the aliens.

The aliens laughed—a deep, horrifying sound.

Zaabha.

Carthago.

House of Galen.

Galen.

Sam felt another burst of pain and squeezed her eyes shut. She tried to hold onto that thought.

"Sam, help me fight!" Blaine yelled.

Galen. Rugged face and eye patch. Black cloak and muscled body. Her Galen.

More pain, like her head was going to explode. When Sam opened her eyes again, Fortuna Station was gone.

Her chest hitched. She was in some huge, cavernous space carved from rock. Ahead lay the entrance to what looked like a maze, with twisting, open tunnels spread as far as she could see. The only light came from the burning torches attached to the walls.

All around her, Galen's gladiators were on their knees, staring sightlessly ahead.

She scrambled onto her feet. *Fuck.* It was some sort of mind-interfering tech. Harper was kneeling closest to Sam, and Sam quickly ran over to the woman.

"Harper." She gripped the woman's shoulder and shook her. "Harper! Snap out of it."

Harper blinked and sucked in a breath. "Sam?"

"You okay?"

"We were on Fortuna?" She looked around, confused. "Aliens were attacking."

"We're on Carthago, Harper. Do you remember?"

The woman blinked again. "Carthago." Then a fierce look crossed her face. "Raiden." She leaped up. "Where's Raiden?"

"Over there." Sam pointed. "Go wake him up."

Kace was next closest to Sam, and she quickly shook him free. His face was covered in sweat, but he nodded at her. They were all being forced to relive nightmares.

She looked around desperately, and spotted Galen. She sprinted to him. He was on his knees, his muscles tensed and veins popping out of his neck.

"Galen." She cupped his cheeks. "Galen."

"Have to save Raiden." His voice was harsh. "Have to save the royal family and Aurelia."

"Galen, it's Sam. We're on Carthago. Come back to me."

His hands clamped down on her arms and he yanked her closer. Suddenly, she was somehow in his memories.

She felt sunshine on her skin and stone pavers

beneath her knees. She looked over her shoulder and gasped.

In front of them, she saw Thraxians fighting with armed guards in rich red uniforms. Galen stared at the fight, face hard. It was a younger Galen, with a handsome face and two glittering-blue eyes. He wasn't in uniform.

"I was hiking in the hills," he whispered. "It was my day off. I left Raiden alone. While I was strolling through the trees, my world was being torn apart."

Her heart clenched. Then Galen raised a sword and leaped into the fight.

Nearby, a very young Raiden was battling with another Thraxian. The ground shook, and Sam looked up. They were outside a beautiful palace, like something out of a fantasy story. But as she watched, a tower toppled, crashing to the ground and breaking into chunks of rock.

Then Raiden stumbled. "Galen!"

The young prince's bodyguard charged toward his young prince, his tattoos flaring blue-green. Sam's gut churned. She knew there was no happy ending for this scenario.

"Your family is dead, boy," the Thraxian yelled at Raiden. "And you're next."

"No!" Enraged, Raiden rushed at the alien.

Galen charged at them. "Raiden, stand down. Get to safety!"

The Thraxian lifted a huge, clawed hand and side-swiped the younger man, sending him flying. Raiden collapsed in a pile and didn't get up.

"No." Galen skewered the Thraxian with his sword.

The Thraxian fought back, swiping at Galen. His claws slashed up Galen's shirt, opening up several deep wounds on Galen's chest.

Pain made Galen's face spasm. He fell back, and the Thraxian fell on top of him.

The Thraxian pushed to his knees, yanking Galen's sword out and throwing it away. Gold blood oozed from his gut wound. Then he roared and gripped Galen's head, his claws hovering right over Galen's left eye.

"You are a failure," the Thraxian said. "I'll make you watch while I gut your young prince."

Emotion poured through Sam as she watched and felt everything Galen was feeling—pain, despair, helplessness.

Galen twisted and jerked, but the Thraxian was heavier and stronger. He had Galen pinned.

The Thraxian kept talking and behind them, another palace tower toppled over.

Then Sam saw the knife in Galen's hand. He was desperately trying to stab it up into the Thraxian, but the Thraxian's arm was long, putting him just out of reach. Galen only needed another inch, and he could sink the knife into his attacker.

Suddenly, Galen went still. Then, before she realized what he planned, his tattoos flared and he reached up with his other hand. He yanked the Thraxian closer.

The Thraxian's claws sank into Galen's eye.

He didn't scream or flinch. Instead, he rammed the knife deep into the Thraxian's chest.

Oh, sweet Lord. "Galen," she said in a broken cry.

Then jarringly, she blinked, and the images dissolved.

Sunlight gave way to flickering shadows. The paved courtyard gave way to an underground cavern.

Galen was on his knees, staring at Sam, the same deep groove in his brow, and agony in his eye. She leaned forward and kissed him.

He blinked.

"Sam?"

"I'm here."

He blinked again and one strong arm snaked around her. He pulled her close. "Sam."

"We're okay, but we have Thraxians to beat."

His face turned to stone. "Thraxians."

She nodded. "It's time to save the day again, boss-man."

GALEN FOCUSED on Sam's eyes, shaking off the past. His gut was churning.

The feel of her warm fingers on his skin helped him pull himself together. He glanced around and saw Harper, Raiden, Kace, and Lore working to wake the others.

His gladiators were all caught in the grip of some strange tech. Galen scowled. He'd seen this before, being tested by insane tech genius Catalyst, and Carthagoan scum, Gabriez. It looked like the Thraxians had made it even stronger.

"Get the rest of them free," he said.

Sam touched his jaw. "You sure you're okay?"

He nodded. "I'm fine now." He pressed his hand over hers. "Help them."

With a nod, she raced off, headed toward Saff.

Slowly, Galen pushed to his feet. Everything hurt. Sam had seen his worst failure. He blew out a breath. She'd seen what had left the scars on his soul.

Shaking it off, he moved to Nero, gripping the man's shoulder. "Wake up, gladiator."

Nero blinked at him, his face set like thunder. "Galen."

"Yes. On your feet, Nero."

Once Nero was up, they moved through the rest of his team, waking them from the tech. Soon, they all stood, white-faced and shaky.

"*Drakking* Thraxians," Thorin snapped. "I'm going to kill them all."

A deep howl echoed around them. They all spun.

"Now what?" Saff yanked a net device off her belt, ready to throw it.

Several beasts slunk out of a dark tunnel, drool dripping from their fang-filled mouths, and their gazes locked on the gladiators.

"This way," Kace yelled.

They all sprinted toward the wide entrance to the maze. It was the only place to go.

"We could take them," Nero yelled.

"There will be more," Galen said.

They headed into the maze tunnels.

"We need a way out," Sam said.

They sprinted through the twisting tunnels. The

walls were carved rock, with several dead ends. Suddenly, a wild screech echoed through the tunnels.

They all stumbled to a halt. Galen heard the pounding of hooves on dirt. More creatures were coming.

"This way," Harper called.

She'd found a small trap door in a side wall. Dropping to her hands and knees, she crawled through it, Raiden right behind her.

They all squeezed through, and came out in another wide, maze tunnel.

As one, they jogged through the twists and turns. But it wasn't long before they were met with a shouting crowd of Zaabha fighters. Swords clashed. Galen rushed forward, slamming his blade against a fighter's sword. Beside him, Thorin swung his axe, and Kace's staff moved in a blur. His gladiators fought hard, and nearby, he saw Sam leap into the air, taking down a fighter.

"Down here," Raiden yelled.

There was an empty tunnel leading away and they followed Raiden, leaving the Zaabha fighters groaning on the rocky ground.

As they turned a corner, Galen's instincts were screaming at him.

"We're being herded," he said.

Sam's face tightened. "You're right. Beasts and fighters popping up and driving us in a certain direction."

Moments later, they broke into a circular space with a sand-covered floor. They all stumbled to a halt.

It looked like an arena, except for a circular hole in the very center of the floor. Vek growled.

"What the *drak*?" Blaine stepped forward. "This reminds me of the underground fight rings."

"What's with the hole?" Raiden asked.

Blaine looked up, his face dark. "Usually something lived in it, and the Srinar liked to feed it losing fighters."

A low, groan-like sound vibrated from the hole.

Sam spun her sword, her gaze on the cavity. Galen watched as a huge, clawed leg came out of the hole, then another and another.

"Fucking hell," Blaine muttered.

Seconds later, an enormous, scaled creature had pulled itself out of the hole.

"What is it?" Sam asked.

"Looks like a killer crab mated with...something bad," Harper said.

The creature had a set of six eyes above a huge mouth, rimmed with sharp teeth.

"I'm not certain, but I believe it's called a *khodor*," Galen said. "Obviously banned from every arena I know."

The animal opened its huge mouth, giving them a view of several rows of jagged teeth. Then suddenly, a black substance sprayed out of its mouth.

The slime hit Nero, slamming the gladiator into the rock wall.

"*Drak!*" He struggled, but the sticky substance held him. Lore rushed to help him.

There was another spray of black and Galen dodged it, slamming into Sam and knocking her out of the way.

The creature screeched, lifting several legs and slamming them down. The ground vibrated under them.

Another spray of black goo caught Saff. With a shout, Blaine rushed to her, hacking away at the sticky, web-like substance with his sword.

Finally, Nero was free, specks of black still stuck to his chest. Lore stepped forward, pulling something off his belt. He tossed something toward the animal.

Fireworks exploded in the creature's face. It let out a loud screech.

"Work together," Galen shouted. "Distract it."

"What are you going to do?" Sam asked.

"Get on it. Find a weak spot."

"Galen." Lore appeared, pressing several pouches into Galen's hands. "Just in case you need them."

"I'm coming with you." Sam slid her sword into her scabbard.

Galen didn't bother arguing with her, just yanked her close for a quick kiss. Then he turned and climbed the maze wall beside him.

Sam followed. The creature was darting in at his gladiators. The gladiators were taunting it—yelling and poking at it with their weapons.

Galen climbed to the top of the wall and balanced precariously on the narrow surface. He helped Sam up beside him.

As the monster moved past them, Galen leaped onto the creature's back. Sam landed beside him. They both gripped the rough scales, the edges biting into their fingers.

"Now what?" Sam looked around. "I don't see any weak spots."

No. The armor-plated scales were tough, and they

completely covered the creature. "We get up to the head and drop one of Lore's pouches inside."

Sam grimaced but nodded. "Let's do it."

They both stood and ran up the beast's back. It moved beneath them, and Sam slipped. Galen reached out and grabbed her hand.

Together, they moved up to the creature's head.

"Galen, look."

From another tunnel, he saw Thraxians and Srinar pouring out into the space below. They were all holding some sort of projectile weapons and shooting at his gladiators.

Galen scowled. He couldn't worry about them right now. First, he and Sam had to bring this creature down. "Come on."

He grabbed one of Lore's pouches and lobbed it towards the creature's mouth.

But as he did, the creature moved, skittering sideways. The pouch hit the edge of the mouth and bounced off. The beast reared, and Galen quickly dropped down and pressed his body to the scales. Sam did the same, holding on as the creature moved beneath them.

"Hold my feet," Sam said.

He frowned. "What?"

"Hold my feet and I'll lean over and get a pouch inside." She held out a hand and Galen set a pouch in it. Then she moved onto her belly and slithered closer to the creature's mouth.

Galen didn't like her plan, but he clamped his hands around her ankles.

She slid closer to the beast's gaping mouth. His gut

hardened. Then she was dangling right over its teeth. She dropped her pouch into its mouth.

Galen quickly pulled her back.

Nothing happened.

"Shit," she muttered. "Galen—"

Thump.

The muffled sound came from inside the creature. A second later, it reared up, screeching wildly. Its legs waved madly.

Galen grabbed Sam as they slid. He yanked her to her feet. "Jump!"

They leaped off. When they hit the ground, they rolled.

A leg slammed down beside them. Galen tackled Sam and they rolled. Another leg rushed at them, and this time, Sam rammed her shoulder into him and they rolled again. The creature teetered away, letting out a mournful groan. Then it finally collapsed.

Thank drak. Galen smiled and heaved in a breath. As he shifted to roll to his feet, he sensed movement beside him.

Only to be met with a sword at his throat.

Sam moved as well, and an axe was pressed to her chest.

Drak. They both looked up and froze.

Galen stared into Raiden's blank face. His one-time charge and prince calmly held his sword at Galen's neck. Beside him, a slack-jawed Thorin lifted his axe, holding it above Sam's head.

"Raiden—" Galen's words faded away.

Both men had silver implants—one on Raiden's neck and another on Thorin's cheek.

"No," Sam breathed.

Galen's hands curled into fists and he quickly glanced at all of his gladiators.

All of them were wearing implants.

CHAPTER FOURTEEN

S am sucked in a horrified breath.

All the House of Galen fighters had implants. On their necks, arms, or faces. She looked at the Thraxians and Srinar and saw that the weapons they were holding could actually shoot the implants.

"Galen," she whispered. "We need to get out of here."

His face was set like stone, a muscle ticking in his temple.

"Bind them," a Thraxian barked.

Nero moved forward, the implant on his arm gleaming dully in the muted light. He was carrying a chain with sturdy cuffs at each end.

He grabbed Sam's arm and snapped the cuff around her wrist. As he tightened it, she glared at the Thraxians. Next, Nero fastened the other end of the chain to Galen. They were now chained together with a few meters of chain between them.

Shit, they needed to do something. Whatever the Thraxians had planned for them, it wouldn't be good.

"Galen."

"We can't leave them." His gaze moved to Raiden.

"We aren't any good to them dead."

She saw the torment on Galen's face. Then he pulled something off his belt. She frowned and watched as he threw it.

A cloud of gray smoke exploded around them. One of Lore's tricks.

Galen grabbed her hand and yanked her up, the chain rattling. Then they ran.

Behind them, she heard shouts. In the smoke, she bumped into someone and heard a grunt. But Galen yanked her on.

"There." She spotted a way out.

They sprinted down the maze tunnel. Sam lifted the chain so it didn't drag and slow them down. They moved through several turns and intersections, arms pumping.

Soon, the sounds of chaos and confusion died away behind them. Finally, they stopped. Sam sucked air into her aching lungs.

Galen pressed a hand to the wall, his face no longer impassive. She felt the fury rolling off him.

"Galen—"

He turned and punched the wall, blood spraying from his knuckles. He punched it again and again.

She grabbed his hand. "Enough."

He tried to pull away, but she held tight.

"I know," she whispered. "I'm here. Hold on to me."

He gritted his teeth and wrapped his arms around her. "We left them. We left Raiden."

"I know." She squeezed him, sharing her strength. "But we're going to rescue them."

"They're under drakking Thraxian control."

"We're going to get them back." She went up on her toes and kissed him, rough and hard. It took a second, but he kissed her back, his fingers clenching on her arms.

"We need to find the scientist and the implant controls," she said. "Zhim said the scientist was here somewhere. He'll know how to disable the implants."

Galen heaved in a breath. "We're in a maze. How the hell will we find him?"

"I don't know. But we won't give up."

She watched him rein in his fury and he nodded. "Let's see if we can get these chains off."

Galen grabbed a rock and smashed at the chain. Sam tugged at her cuff.

It was no use. They were too sturdy, specially designed to hold unwilling prisoners.

"Forget it," she said. "Let's get moving."

Together, they turned and moved deeper into the maze. With the chain tethering them together, it took them a few minutes to work out how to run while linked. The burning torches made light and shadows dance. The maze was eerily empty, but occasionally she heard moans and the distant sound of fighting.

Galen was brooding and she knew he was thinking of his people.

The Thraxians thrived on hurting and enslaving others. Sam didn't understand how they could do that with no conscience—she'd spent so many nights, nursing her wounds and wondering about it. But it didn't matter what had turned the alien species so uncaring and bloodthirsty, this had to end. They had to rescue their friends.

"Galen." The static-filled crackle came from Galen's belt.

He reached down and snatched the communicator. "Zhim?"

There was another crackle.

"... Connect... Can you hear...?"

"I can barely hear you. We're underground. Where are you?"

"... Ryan... Rillian."

"We need to find the scientist," Galen said. "My gladiators have been implanted. All of them. We have to help them."

"Scientist signal... Center... Above."

Suddenly, the communicator cut off and Galen cursed.

"Center above," Sam murmured.

"Zhim and the others must be up in Zaabha," Galen said. "We need to get out of here and back to the surface."

Sam wasn't so sure. She moved to the rock wall and gripped it. "Let's climb up and see what we can see." She rattled the chain. "I need you to come with me."

He gave her a brusque nod. Together, they quickly scaled the wall, finally crouching on top of it.

Sam glanced toward the center of the maze. *Dios*, there were so many tunnels. Her gaze fell on a towering column of rock in the heart of the maze. The maze circled around it in a dizzying array of open tunnels. She looked up, taking in the tower's rocky surface.

Then she spotted something. "Galen, look."

High up on the rock tower, close to where it met the surface, were a bank of windows.

Galen cursed. "They're *drakking* watching us."

"Like rats in a maze. The scientist must be up there. Center above."

"Time for a climb." Galen stood on top of the wall. Sam followed suit.

The walls were wide enough to allow them to walk on top of them, rather than down in the maze. This way, they could easily see where they needed to go. Once they determined the walls were sturdy and could easily hold them, they picked up the pace and started to jog.

Finally, they reached the end of the wall.

"We need to jump." Galen pulled their chain closer. "Together."

She nodded. "On three."

"One. Two. Three."

They threw themselves across the gap. Sam landed on the next wall, bending her knees. Galen crouched, gripping the edge.

He shot her a small smile. "No one else I'd prefer to be chained to in the middle of a deadly maze."

She smiled back. "You say the sweetest things, Imperator Galen."

They kept running. In one tunnel, they spotted several Zaabha fighters. The group, dressed in ragged clothes, looked up and shouted in surprise.

"Get them!" one man bellowed.

As the fighters tried to climb the wall, Galen and Sam kicked them back.

"Keep moving," he called out.

Sam jumped over the grasping hands and kept moving behind Galen.

But before too long, the walls narrowed until they were too thin for them to walk on. Dammit, they were so close. She could see the tower only about twenty meters away. Galen nodded at the ground.

They both jumped, landing on the rocky floor.

"This way," he said.

They ran down one tunnel, but it finished at a dead end. Galen shook his head. They turned and headed back.

"That one," she said, pointing. The tower rose up above them, taunting them. So close.

They kept jogging and Sam thought about the others, praying they were okay. Suddenly, Galen stopped, and Sam almost collided with him. She looked up, her heart thumping against her ribs.

The base of the tower was right in front of them.

Sam grinned. "Made it."

Then a ragtag group of fighters appeared, all holding rocks and makeshift weapons.

Sam's hands curled. *Dammit.* They all looked malnourished and desperate. She didn't want to kill them.

Then a woman stepped forward, her long hair tangled around her face. "You came back."

Sam tilted her head. It was one of the workers from the engine room on Zaabha. She glanced around, seeing other soot-lined faces. "I told you we would." She looked at Galen. "The imperator always keeps his promises."

Something moved over Galen's face. "First, we plan to take care of the Thraxians, then we're getting you all out of here and back to Kor Magna."

There were cheers and sobs. The crowd stepped back.

A young man nodded at them. "Good luck."

Galen looked down at Sam. "Now we climb."

***

GALEN GRIPPED the rock and pulled himself upward. He grunted and heard the damn chain clank as Sam climbed up beside him.

Whatever it took, he was getting his people back.

But he wasn't alone.

He turned to look at Sam. *His*. A warrior who fought at his side, who put her arms around him when he needed it. He had a woman who was strength and softness. A woman who would bend, but never break. The Thraxians had tried to break her, but instead, they'd just strengthened her.

Sam was a woman he could count on and lean on. One who gave him things he never knew he needed.

One of his boots slipped. He bit back a curse and quickly pressed himself against the rock. If he fell, Sam would plummet with him.

"Okay?" she asked.

"Yeah." He got a firmer foothold and kept moving.

With a smile, she moved past him, climbing like she did it every day.

"You're enjoying the climb," he said.

"I used to rock climb on my vacations back on Earth. It's fun."

Galen snorted. "I think we can disagree on that."

"Well, I do prefer a safety harness, as opposed to being chained to my climbing partner—"

Suddenly, a projectile thumped into the rock beside Galen.

He jerked and Sam gasped. A black, metal bolt was lodged into the stone.

Galen looked down and saw several Thraxians at the base of the tower. They were all aiming crossbows at him and Sam.

"Sam, climb faster!"

She nodded and moved upward, her muscles flexing. Galen followed.

Thunk. Thunk. Thunk.

Bolts peppered the wall. Grimly, Galen held on and kept climbing. He felt like a *drakking* target in the training arena.

Another bolt hit close to Sam. She cried out, her hands slipping off the rock.

She fell.

Galen lunged after the chain. He gripped it hard with one hand, clinging to the rock with his other hand and his boots. He gritted his teeth and met her gaze. Her face was white as she hung there.

"I've got you," he said.

"I know."

Perfect trust in her tone. He pulled her up until she could reach the wall again. She gripped it, pressing flat against it.

"Shit." She pulled in a breath. "Thanks."

More projectiles hit the wall.

"Keep going."

They climbed steadily, and the next round of projectiles hit below their feet.

"We're out of range," he said.

"Thank God." Sam arched her neck. "And we're almost at the windows. Look."

He saw the windows not far above them. "Let's do this."

He wasn't leaving his people as enslaved prisoners any longer than necessary. Galen and Sam closed the distance, stopping just below the window.

"How do we break the glass?" she asked. "Sword hilt?"

He hefted the chain. "I have a better idea."

She smiled and nodded. Together, they swung the chain at the glass.

Crack.

Galen saw the spiderweb crack form. They swung it again.

The window shattered.

"Now!" Galen pushed himself through the window.

Sam followed him in. They both leaped to their feet in time to see several Thraxians running toward them.

Then Sam looked at him and smiled. At the same time, they both reached over their shoulders and pulled their swords.

"For honor and freedom," Galen said.

"For honor and freedom!" Sam yelled.

Galen swung high and Sam dropped low. She swiped out with her leg, toppling the closest Thraxian. Then she was slicing upward with her sword. Galen tugged on the chain, yanking her up with extra momentum.

Then he turned and slashed his sword at another Thraxian. He swiveled, his blade hitting against another Thraxian's sword.

Sam leaped into the air, pulling hard on the chain. Galen moved closer to her and watched as she gripped a Thraxian by the arm, bent down, and tossed the alien over her shoulder.

"Sam." He lifted the chain, and she nodded.

Together, they ran, slamming the chain into two Thraxians. Then Sam jumped up, twisting, and the chain wrapped around the aliens. They fell in a tumble of arms and legs. Galen followed with his sword, pouring all his burning fury into the fight. Soon, all the Thraxians were down on the ground, dead or groaning in their death throes.

In front of them, cowering by a large bench, was a tall, thin Thraxian, wearing a long, silver robe. The scientist.

And sitting in the center of the bench, resting on the metallic holder, was a white crystal cube.

CHAPTER FIFTEEN

S am advanced on the scientist, and Galen stood behind her.

She glared at the alien. "Remember me?"

The Thraxian took a step back.

"How do we deactivate the implants?" she demanded.

Galen fought back a smile. *Drak*, she was tough. The Thraxian scientist didn't respond, and Galen raised his sword.

The alien swallowed, his gaze flickering from Sam's hard face, to Galen's sword, then to the crystal on the bench.

"The crystal?" Sam said. "It controls the implants as well as storing data about them?"

The Thraxian gave a reluctant nod, his dark eyes burning. "You'll never get out of here alive."

"It ends today," Galen said. "Right here. No more

hurting people. No more imprisoning people. No more suffering."

Clearly out of patience, Sam lunged. At the last second, the scientist lifted something he had hidden in his robe and fired.

The implant hit Sam in the shoulder. She stumbled back.

Galen leaped forward. "Sam!" He swung his sword, but the scientist dropped to the floor, his projectile weapon clattering to the tiles.

"Please—" The Thraxian stumbled back, lifting his hands to shield himself.

Galen held the sword on the man's throat. "Did all your victims beg? When you stuck implants in their bodies and experimented on them? Did you grant them mercy?"

A weight hit Galen, tackling him to the ground. He turned and saw Sam on him, pinning him down. Her face was blank, her empty gaze on him.

No. He pressed a hand to her chest, trying to keep her off him and stop her from hurting herself.

The doors to the room whooshed open, and more Thraxians rushed inside.

"Secure him," the lead Thraxian yelled.

Sam rose and Galen was jerked to his feet.

"Sam?" His gut churned. "Fight it."

No response. She looked over his shoulder at the wall.

The lead Thraxian stepped in front of him, an orange sash across his chest. "You failed, Imperator Galen."

Galen just glared at him.

"The great Galen is not so great after all." The man bared ugly, black teeth. "All your people are now my slaves. I'll take your House, and everything you value."

Galen lifted his chin, grinding his teeth together. Inside, the Thraxian's words tore him up.

The Thraxian stepped closer. "You failed. Just as you failed to save your royal family and your planet."

The words were a hard blow. They carved out his insides and Galen bowed his head. Everything the Thraxian said was true. He had failed Raiden's family and his planet. Nothing, no accomplishment, no amount of wealth, would ever change that.

The Thraxian drew a large, jagged knife off his belt. It was a dark black that absorbed the light.

He handed it to Sam. "Kill him, Champion of Zaabha."

Her fingers closed around the hilt of the knife. It looked huge in her smaller hand. She moved toward Galen, her movements robotic.

He watched her come. His Sam, his woman. The woman he loved.

The emotion stormed through him. He'd realized too late. "I'm so sorry, Sam."

She pressed the tip of his knife against his gut. He waited for her to shove it deep, his gaze on her face.

Then she winked at him.

SAM FOUGHT the compulsion of the implant from taking her over.

She felt like electricity was buzzing through her, making her muscles twitch, but since the implant had hit her, she'd been able to fight off the implant's control. Her only guess was that the previous implant experiment had given her some sort of immunity. She'd tackled Galen earlier to keep up the ruse.

But as she winked at him, she saw his eye twitch. That was it. Her tough, smart imperator didn't give anything away.

"You aren't alone," she whispered.

"I love you." His words were near soundless.

Something burst inside her chest. This remarkable man, a man she'd found at her lowest point, loved her. "I love you too."

Sam moved the knife, spinning it and pressing the hilt into his hand.

"Duck," he said.

She dropped and saw Galen throw the knife.

It hit the lead Thraxian in the neck. Orange blood sprayed and, with a gurgle, the alien collapsed.

Sam spun and jumped up, hitting the closest Thraxian. As he fell, she grabbed his staff and then, whirling, she attacked.

Beside her, Galen was grappling hand-to-hand with another Thraxian.

Together, still linked by their chain, they worked their way through the aliens, hitting, kicking, spinning. She smiled. They were almost all down. They had this.

Then the doors opened, and more Thraxians and Srinar flooded in. Several were holding large crossbows.

No. Sam stumbled.

Thwap. Thwap. Thwap.

She saw Galen's body jerk. For a second, she thought they'd hit him with an implant, as well.

But then she saw it was worse. Far worse. A wicked, black bolt was lodged in his shoulder, and another in his gut.

"No!" She leaped forward.

Galen went down on one knee. A Thraxian stepped over him, aiming the crossbow right at him.

Sam threw herself over Galen's prone body. She'd already lost everyone she loved. She wasn't losing Galen as well.

She cupped his cheeks, and her heart clenched at the pain etched on his face. And blood. *Dios*, there was so much blood.

"Sam...move."

His voice was raspy and lacking its usual commanding strength.

"Never." She felt tears stream down her cheeks. "Not alone, remember?"

She heard a sound and looked up. The Thraxian towering over her had the crossbow aimed at her.

"You lose." The Thraxian smirked. "Long live the House of Thrax."

Sam tightened her hold on Galen and felt him slide an arm around her.

Suddenly, the windows exploded inward. Glass flew everywhere, like a shower of deadly rain.

Sam curled around Galen, and heard the Thraxians and Srinar shouting. When she looked up, she saw several muscled bodies fly through the broken windows.

Men landed inside, all of them crouched. Then they rose.

The man in the lead had a silver arm and implant around his neon-blue eye. *Magnus Rone.*

Beside him stood a grim-faced, silver-furred Tano, holding a weapon in each of his four hands—House of Zeringei. Next to him was a man wearing a leather harness and a green cloak—House of Loden. Another gladiator flanked Magnus wearing blue, fish-scale armor —House of Man'u. On the other side of him, stood a massive fighter dressed all in black with a skull logo on his shoulder and a face that looked hewn from rock— House of Mortas.

Behind them spread out a line of fierce looking fighters of different species. All of them held weapons— swords, staffs, axes.

The imperators of Kor Magna had arrived.

GALEN FORCED DOWN HIS PAIN, watching as the imperators burst into action.

Through the windows behind them, Magnus' cyborgs climbed inside with powerful flexes of their bodies. They were followed by Rillian's black-clad soldiers, and several gladiators from the other houses.

Fighting broke out all around them.

"Sam," he croaked. "The crystal."

She looked down at him, torn.

"Go. Disable it."

She nodded. "I don't think I can reach it. The chain isn't long enough."

Galen summoned all the strength he had left. He'd never let anything stop him, especially when it came to protecting his people. He heaved himself up, feeling the sticky slide of his own blood. Pain exploded through him and he almost blacked out.

"So damn stubborn." Sam curled an arm around him, and together, they shuffled toward the lab bench.

When she set him back down, Galen collapsed, feeling nauseated.

"I'll be right back," she said.

With his vision wavering, he watched her grab the crystal off the stand. Then she spun and faced the Thraxian scientist, cowering behind the bench.

With two long strides, she reached him and yanked him up. "Show me how to deactivate it."

Heedless of the blood sliding down his body, Galen smiled. Getting on the wrong side of his Earth woman was a bad idea.

His mind urged him to get up, to help her, but he trusted Sam. He trusted his allies. Besides, he wasn't sure he could get up again.

With shaking hands, the Thraxian showed Sam what to do. Then, while she was occupied, the Thraxian made a run for it.

"Hey!" Sam cried. She lunged for him, but missed grabbing his robe by a whisper.

The scientist sprinted close to the windows, trying to skirt the fighting and reach the door. Suddenly, a spear from one of the Loden gladiators hit the Thraxian. It stabbed through his stomach, and he staggered.

With wide eyes, he stumbled closer to the windows. He hit the edge and tumbled backward and out the window with a scream.

Galen couldn't summon any pity for the man.

Sam kneeled beside Galen. "The crystal's powered down." She pressed it into his hand.

Galen tightened his fingers around it...then he crushed it into shards.

"Galen." Magnus appeared, his eye glowing neon blue.

"Good to see you, Magnus." Galen coughed and tasted blood on his lips.

The cyborg nodded, then called out to the others. "Round up the Thraxians and Srinar."

"And the captives," Galen said. "Free them, and get the Earth women to help. They have a softer touch...and they understand."

Magnus nodded again.

Sam pressed a cloth to Galen's wounds. "You're losing too much blood."

He knew that. He felt his strength slipping away. "Whatever happens, take care of the House of Galen and its people."

Her lips pressed into a flat line. "That's your job."

"Sam—"

"No, damn you. You've survived this fucking long." She leaned closer. "You are not going to die on me." Her voice lowered, her eyes swimming with pain. "Please."

He felt something in his chest ache.

"You deserve to live, Galen. You deserve to be happy."

The doors opened again, causing all the imperators to spin around and lift their weapons.

Galen saw his House of Galen people flood inside.

Their faces were lined with anger. Thorin looked ready to explode. Galen slumped with a flood of relief. They were no longer under the control of the implants.

Raiden went down on one knee beside Galen and Sam. The gladiator was bloody and covered in scrapes, his red cloak in tatters, but he was alive. Harper stood at his side.

"Leave you alone for a bit and look what happens." Raiden's tone was light, but there was concern on his face.

"I'm too stubborn to die." Galen looked up at Sam. "And I have a very good reason not to die."

She managed a shaky smile and cupped his cheek. He felt the warmth of the touch right through him. "If you want more of my sweet rolls, you'd better not die."

Then Galen looked over his people. Nero and Thorin had joined the other fighters in chaining up the Thraxians and Srinar. "Everyone's okay?"

"Scrapes and bruises," Raiden said. "They're fine."

"He needs medical help," Sam said. "Now."

Magnus appeared again. "It's on its way."

A moment later, the door opened once more. Rillian and Dayna—both wearing black body armor—stepped inside. Behind them, a medical team rushed in, Winter among them.

"Winter," Nero growled.

"Rillian brought us," she said.

Galen counted several healers, from multiple Houses.

"We had a full team of soldiers protecting us, barbarian." Winter went up on her toes and pressed a kiss to Nero's jaw. Then she rushed to Galen.

Galen felt a pressure injector against his neck. Winter's face was focused as she nudged Sam out of the way. "Let's get you fixed up, Galen."

"That would be appreciated, Winter."

"Shh. Don't talk." The woman opened her medical kit.

Sam squeezed Galen's hand. "It's over."

"Yes." He watched her looking around. "Any surviving Thraxians and their allies will be banished to the ShadeFury mines for the rest of their lives."

There were several sharp gasps.

Magnus nodded. "The ShadeFury mines are a deserving punishment."

"The mines are not a fun place," Galen said. "And Zaabha will be dismantled."

Sam smiled, and then leaned down to kiss him. "Zaabha is at an end, but other things are just beginning."

Galen hoped so. He absorbed the taste of her, wanting to pull her closer and carry her off somewhere private.

Winter probed one of his wounds and Galen groaned. "All I want is you in my bed, and no interruptions for several days."

Winter giggled.

Sam grinned, her nose pressed to his. "I think that can be arranged, boss-man."

The Imperator of the House of Aviar stood nearby. The big man shook his head. "What is it about these Earth women?"

CHAPTER SIXTEEN

S am didn't want to be anywhere else.

She was lying in Galen's big bed, pressed up against his warm, hard body. She slid her hands down his chest and over the ridges of his belly. His now-healed body.

He was asleep, and she took the moment to explore him. She wouldn't easily forget seeing him, horribly injured, with a pool of blood forming around him.

She wouldn't easily forget the fear that she might lose him.

Sam circled his hardening cock, stroking it.

He woke with a jolt. *"Buenas tardes."*

She smiled at her man. He kept surprising her with some Spanish. "It's a very good evening."

For three days they'd mostly stayed in Galen's bedroom, resting, eating, and making love. Yes, everything was pretty darn perfect.

She pressed a kiss to his chest, right over where the

bolt had pierced him. It had been close to the slash scars he'd kept for so many years. Her chest filled with warmth. He'd finally allowed the Medical team to heal both his new wounds and the old scars.

"How are you feeling?" she asked.

"Like I'm the luckiest man in the galaxy." His hand slid into her hair. "Like I love you more and more every day."

"*Dios*, I love you too, Galen. Your strength, your protectiveness, your sense of right and wrong."

"*Te amo*," he murmured.

Her life had been destroyed, like his had, but now she felt like the pieces were coming back together. Maybe with some scars that would never quite fade, but those scars helped make them stronger. Helped them appreciate what they had. Glowing with happiness, Sam kissed him.

"I'm feeling the urge to get creative," he murmured against her lips.

Her belly spasmed. Over the last few days, Galen had proven that he could get *very* creative when he was in the mood. And when he did, it usually ended with her screaming.

She could hardly believe that Zaabha was gone. That the House of Thrax no longer existed, and all remaining Thraxians that had been involved with Zaabha had been rounded up. She knew they were headed to their new life at the ShadeFury mines.

Zaabha's prisoners had been freed, and she knew Madeline had been working overtime coordinating with the other houses to help get the former captives home.

The nightmare was over, and now they had to get on with living.

She stroked Galen's cock again and he groaned. She smiled. She really liked having him at her mercy.

Suddenly, the bedroom door burst open. Galen cursed and Sam yanked the sheet up over their naked bodies.

"Okay, you guys have been here for *days*," Rory complained. She had Finley on her hip.

Regan stood shyly beside her. "Sorry to interrupt."

Madeline bustled across the room. When she reached the windows, she yanked open the curtains.

Harper stood in the doorway, grinning unrepentantly. "There's a party planned. All the Houses are coming, and you two are the guests of honor."

"So out of bed." Mia strode in, holding a dress. "This is for you, Sam."

Hero jumped onto the bed, walking around in circles like he was looking for a place to sit.

Galen growled.

Sam laughed, dropping her head to his shoulder. "Do you regret taking in these Earth women?"

He gripped her hip. "Never."

Sam sat up. "All right, you guys. You got our attention. Out!"

The women headed for the door, Finley cooing. Hero bounded off the bed to follow. Rory was last out, winking at them as she closed the door.

"Time for a shower." Galen scooped Sam up.

She leaned into his hold, feeling his hard cock brush

against her. "I don't think getting clean is the only thing on your mind, Imperator."

"No." His voice deepened. "I have some very dirty things planned as well."

He carried her under the spray and a moment later, his slick hands cupped her breasts. She moaned. Any touch from him and she felt like her body went up in flames.

"You look good wet," he murmured.

"You look good all the time."

Her back hit the tiles and his hands cupped her ass. As she wrapped her legs around his hips, his thick cock thrust inside her.

Pinned to the tiles, she cried out.

"That's it." His deep voice vibrated in her ear. "I want to hear you scream my name."

"Make me," she breathed.

He pounded deep, his face hard and intense. He looked down at their connected bodies. "Drak, Sam, I love watching you. I love seeing you take me. I love being joined to you."

Pleasure was a violent tidal wave washing over her. Her nails bit into his shoulders. "Don't stop."

"Never."

She thrust back against him as much as she could. "Don't stop."

"Now, Sam."

An order she was happy to obey. Her screams echoed off the tiles. Then he spilled inside her with a deep groan, lowered his head and bit that special, sensitive spot on her neck. Sam felt another pulse of pleasure and cried out again.

Galen left her feeling flushed and happy as he headed back to the bedroom to get dressed. She watched that tight, muscled ass of his as he left and sighed. All hers.

She dried her hair and in the mirror, she saw the dark mark on her neck. She smiled. Every time it looked like it was starting to fade, he bit her again. He was possessive, but never made her feel like a possession. She used some of the makeup the women had left for her. She accentuated the golden glow of her skin and did some smoky eyes. Then she turned to the dress Mia had brought for her. It hung on the back of the bathroom door.

Sam hadn't really looked at it before, and now she gasped. She *loved* it.

Quickly, she slipped it on. She turned to face the mirror, the skirt sliding around her legs. The dress was red and silver. House of Galen colors.

The silver beaded bodice clung to her torso, giving an almost armor-like effect. Red, silky fabric flowed down to the floor, long slits on either side giving glimpses of her legs.

She walked out of the bathroom and her breath caught in her throat.

Galen turned from contemplating the view out the window. A fierce, possessive look crossed his face.

Sam guessed her face looked the same. *Mine. All mine.*

He was wearing his trademark black cloak, but there

was no black shirt covering his torso. His hard chest and chiseled abs were on display, as were all his tattoos.

"So damn handsome." She walked toward him.

He closed the distance, his arm circling her. "So *drakking* beautiful." He leaned down and nuzzled her neck. "I love seeing you in my colors."

"Ready to celebrate, my imperator?"

"Yes." He offered her his arm.

She linked her arm through his and they headed out. They walked through the corridors of the House of Galen, passing several workers, who smiled broadly at them. When he smiled back at them, Sam saw surprised, pleased looks on their faces.

As they neared the training arena, she heard the sound of music and lots of voices.

Then they stepped outside.

Sam smiled. The training arena had been transformed. Lights were strung up everywhere, and in the center of the arena, round lanterns appeared to float in the night sky. Mingling bodies filled the arena and the arched walkways surrounding it. She could see people from all the Houses. Workers moved through the crowd with loaded trays of food and drink.

Galen pulled her forward and the crowd parted. Right in the center, the House of Galen gladiators and their partners stood, smiles on their faces.

They all lifted their glasses to Sam and Galen.

She looked up and saw emotion working over Galen's face. He was looking at Raiden, who was standing with Harper.

The men shared a look that Sam knew held so much.

Her hand tightened on Galen. It was an acknowledgment that Galen's job was done.

Then Galen's blue gaze moved over all his gladiators, and the women who'd captured their hearts and enriched their lives.

Nearby, Rillian stood, elegant as ever, with Dayna tucked against his side. Beside them were Zhim and Ryan, Corsair and Neve, and Magnus and Ever, holding their baby Asha.

"Your family," she murmured.

Galen nodded. Then he looked down at her. "My world."

Sam threw her arms around his neck and kissed him, right there in front of everyone.

Cheers erupted all around them.

"Okay, enough of that," Rory called out. "Let's get this party started."

Sam found herself pulled away from Galen, and a drink shoved in her hand. She met dozens of people whose names she couldn't remember.

Finally, she stood with her friends, sipping her drink. She watched a bare-chested Kace walk past with Finley strapped to his torso.

"That man is hot," Sam said.

Rory sighed. "I know. So is yours."

Sam followed Rory's gaze to Galen. He was sitting in a chair that had been set up at the edge of the party. A blue-haired young woman was leaning over him, using some sort of machine to add more tattoos to his body. Apparently, she was Raiden's tattoo artist.

Galen's gaze met Sam's, and she shoved her drink at

Rory. That icy gaze glittered with a heat that was all for her. She was addicted and didn't care. As she walked toward him, she heard Rory laughing.

The tattoo artist smiled. "Almost finished."

"Thanks, Vessa." Galen held out a hand to Sam.

She took it and looked down at Galen's body and gasped.

The new ink graced part of his chest and side. It looked gorgeous on his bronze skin, and her heart squeezed. The tattoo on his chest was her face, set with fierce concentration. There was another image, too, of both of them fighting together inked over his ribs. They had their swords raised. And another tattoo of the two of them that Vessa was just finishing—Sam standing in Galen's arms, their gazes locked, looking like they were about to kiss.

Her throat went tight. "They're beautiful, Galen. I love you."

"All finished." Vessa stood. "I think I deserve a drink. This is some of my best work." She gave them a nod and headed toward the drinks table.

"You're it for me, Sam." Galen stood and pulled her close, holding her just like the image that was etched on his skin. "Your body, your hair, your eyes. Your scent, your taste." His hands slid down her body. "Your strength." He rested his palms over her belly. "One day this might swell with our child. Every day, I will stand proudly by your side. One day, we'll grow old, and even when my hair is all gray, I will still be here, your heart, your shield, yours."

Emotion burst through Sam, and tears pricked her

eyes. "When I look at you, Galen, I see strength, honor, and courage. When I look at you, I see the rest of my life."

Raiden

RAIDEN SMILED as he watched Galen and Sam, lost in each other. He recognized the look on his friend's face. *Love.*

Turning his head, Raiden glanced across the crowd to find his own woman. His gaze found Harper instantly, drawn to her. His warrior, his gladiator, his heart. Inside, he felt the deepest contentment, something he hadn't felt since he was a child. She'd helped fill the holes inside him.

Harper turned, and when she saw him watching her, a smile lit her face. Her dress left one toned shoulder bare, and he saw the ink on her skin. His mark. He had matching tattoos on his own skin, all dedicated to the Earth woman he loved.

But that ink was nowhere as indelible as the mark she'd left on his heart.

Thorin

THORIN LISTENED to Regan's giggle. She was

laughing at something Rory had said and was pressed firmly against his side.

The sound of her laugh and the feel of her warmed his insides. She was his heart. She'd accepted him completely as he was, all of him.

His sweet Earth girl.

That such a small thing—her head barely reached his shoulder—could bring him to his knees should have worried him. But it didn't. He was grateful every day to have Regan in his life.

She looked up at him, her eyes luminous. No, she didn't just accept him, she gloried in loving him. He slid his big hand around her hip and splayed his fingers over her belly. They'd discovered today that he'd planted a child inside her.

Emotions worked through him—a blend of exhilaration, fear, and excitement. She smiled. They hadn't shared their secret with anyone, yet. It was theirs for a little while longer before they shared it with their friends and family.

A child made in love.

A child Thorin would protect with his life.

A child who would be the best of both of them.

Kace

KACE LISTENED to his wife roar with laughter. Rory did everything at one hundred percent. Her work, her friendships, being a mother, and loving him. She threw herself into life with a lust and gusto he never tired of watching.

He stroked her shining red hair, and she turned and blew him a kiss. As she went back to talking to her friends, Kace looked down at the baby snuggled to his chest.

Kace's son looked up at him—sweet, precious, and innocent. Finley had his mother's green eyes, but Kace also saw himself in the shape of his child's face and his sturdy, little body.

Once, Kace had only believed himself a weapon, incapable of much else. But Rory had changed that. One bold woman from Earth had given Kace everything. She loved him fiercely, and she'd taught him how to love her back.

"We are very lucky, little man."

Finley gurgled and gave his father a gummy grin.

Lore

LORE WATCHED as his wife moved through the crowd. She was so beautiful and elegant, his *dushla*.

Madeline's gown was a slender column of midnight blue that accented her slim curves. It had been one of Lore's proudest moments when he'd taken this woman as his. They'd shared their joining ceremony over the comm line to Earth with her son.

"You'd love her, Yelena," he whispered to the sister he'd lost so long ago.

Lore saw Madeline was checking in with the House of Galen workers, ensuring the party was running smoothly. Always working. Only he could coax her into letting loose. Only he knew how deeply she really cared and loved.

And only he got to see that hidden fire of hers that was only for him.

Lore set his drink down and smiled. Time to coax his wife into a dark corner for some stolen kisses.

Blaine

BLAINE RAN his hands up Saff's long, sleek body. He fused his mouth with hers, swallowing her moan.

God, he would never get enough of this woman. His woman.

She undulated against him. "Need you inside me, Earth man."

They were in an empty corridor inside the House of Galen, hidden in the shadows. He'd backed her up against the wall, one of her long legs hitched over his hip.

Saff's hand fumbled at the fastenings of his trousers.

From nearby, he heard the noise of the party. "Someone might—"

"Doesn't matter." She bit down on his lip, drawing blood.

Blaine's control slipped, and he pushed her higher until her long legs wrapped around his hips. He didn't have to push the short hem of her sexy, little dress far to bare her to him.

"God, I love you." She was his strength, his heart, his partner in every sense of the word.

Her face softened. "Love you too, Earth-man."

Blaine hated what the Thraxians had done—destroying Fortuna and the lives of so many—but what's done was done, and he knew in his heart that he wouldn't change a thing. He was supposed to have Saff in his life. He was a better man with his fierce gladiator by his side.

She nipped his ear. "Now hurry."

"Yes, ma'am."

Nero

NERO FOUND his woman in Medical. *No surprise.* "Winter, there's a party going on."

She spun, her gold-colored skirts flaring out around her. Pretty as ever, and as always, his body reacted to the sight of her.

Her dark hair was down, his favorite style, and her bi-colored eyes were always fascinating. He even liked the vision device at her temple—it was a part of her now too. He could look at her all day.

"I know, I know." She held up a hand. "I just had to check on a patient."

Nero gripped her arm. "Party. Now."

She huffed out a breath. "Bossy."

But she followed him as they exited Medical. "I never

thought I'd see the day when Nero Krahn was in a hurry to get back to a party."

Nero leaned down and swept her into his arms, holding her tight against his chest. She gasped, a smile on her lips, and slid her arm across his shoulders.

He brushed his lips against hers. "I'd be happy to find something else for us to do."

Smiling, she cupped his jaw. "There's the barbarian gladiator I know and love."

Love. It pounded through Nero, all for this small woman from a distant planet called Earth.

"Your barbarian." *Always.*

"Yes, you are." She pressed her mouth to his.

Vek

VEK HUNCHED HIS SHOULDERS. The lights of the party were too bright. There was too much noise and too many people.

Everyone seemed to be having a good time celebrating the end of Zaabha and the Thraxians. He looked over at his Mia. She was swaying her hips to the music and sipping her drink.

As always, shocked pleasure ran through him. She was his, and every day he was amazed by her. He watched the lights glint off her golden hair.

Vek wanted to scoop up his mate and slip off to the rooftop garden. He'd stalk her through the trees and love her under the moonlight. *His Mia.* She was like a song to his soul. She'd given him his freedom and given him her love. She'd made him the man that he was today.

It didn't matter that her skin was pink and his was blue, that she was from Earth and he didn't even remember his planet, they were a perfect match.

She spotted him looking at her and came over to him, a soft smile on her face. Vek knew many people hesitated to even get close to him. But without hesitation, she wrapped her arms around him.

"Want to sneak off?" There was a glint in her eye.

His gut churned. Ever since Rory had given birth, Mia had decided she wanted babies. Even knowing that Vek's species gave birth to multiple younglings at once hadn't deterred her. But Vek was big and Mia was so small, and it made him nervous. He'd never let any harm come to her.

But as his mate smiled at him, Vek knew he was doomed, because whatever his Mia wanted, he'd move the entire planet to give it to her.

CHAPTER SEVENTEEN

Zhim

Z him tossed back his drink, savoring the burn. His gaze was locked on Ryan.

Did her dress have to be so *drakking* short?

She was talking with Dayna, waving her arms as she spoke. The tiny black dress—the same color as her hair—was covered in shimmering beads and left most of her slim legs bare.

He was itching to know what she had on under the dress. She'd teased him about it before they'd left their penthouse to come to the party.

A surprise for you to uncover later, info-boy. Well, Zhim hated surprises.

Enough. He strode over and spun her into his arms. She gasped and he pressed a hard kiss to her mouth.

"Well, hello there, info-boy." She grinned at him, narrowly avoiding spilling her drink.

"You're driving me crazy."

She smiled. "That is my goal in life."

He growled, which only made her smile widen.

"Want to dance?" she asked.

"Not vertically."

Her eyelashes fluttered, and the heart she'd brought back to life clenched in his chest. *Drak*, he loved her. He wondered how he'd ever survived without Ryan in his life. She challenged him, met him toe-to-toe, and made him laugh.

She went up on her toes, fiddling with his long hair. "Luckily for you, I've made a new list."

He stiffened, heat shooting through him. Ryan enjoyed making lists of all the things she wanted to try.

Her lips brushed his ear. "I added lots of new sex positions that I want to test out."

Zhim grabbed her drink and set it down on the table. "No more drinks. I want you sober when I fuck you."

Ryan tipped her head back and laughed. "Deal."

Corsair

CORSAIR KEPT one arm wrapped around Neve. They both watched her sister coo at her baby.

"She's happy," Neve said.

Corsair heard the happiness in his woman's voice. He knew how much she loved her sister. How much she'd risked for Ever.

"She is." He paused. "Do you want one?"

"One what?" Neve frowned, then her head jerked, her pale-green eyes going wide. "A *baby*?"

Corsair hid his smile at her panic and stroked her dark, curly hair. "Yes."

"Ahh...one day, I guess. But not now." Her arm tightened on him. "I'm happy with just me and my man."

He was as well. He could picture a child they'd make together—dark hair and pale-green eyes. There was no doubt in his heart that Neve would be a fierce, protective, and loving mother. One day.

Across the crowd, he saw his two best friends, Mersi and Bren. Mersi had cleaned up well. He was so used to seeing her in her desert gear that the pretty purple dress was a surprise. She was smiling at a lean, bare-chested gladiator from the House of Davon. She laughed and the gladiator smiled. He was clearly flirting with her. Bren stood nearby, scowling at them.

A second later, Bren strode across the space, grabbed Mersi's arm, and yanked her away.

Uh-oh. Corsair had always known this trouble would come to a head eventually. Neve pressed a hand to his chest and he lost sight of his friends. He blew out a breath. They had to work it out themselves.

He looked down into Neve's gorgeous face. "Do you want to dance?"

She shot him a slightly horrified look. "No."

"Want to make out?"

Her eyes flashed. "Now you're talking, my desert rogue."

Corsair pulled her closer, breathing deep and drawing in the scent of her. It moved through him, and he

205

felt the same sense of peace and completion he did when he watched the sun rise over the desert dunes.

So wild and fierce. And his.

Rillian

RILLIAN HANDED DAYNA A DRINK. She accepted it with a smile.

She was wearing a sleek column of gold, her hair swept up in a style that left her long neck bare. He was a man with more wealth than he could count, who could buy and sell anything he wanted, but as always, he was thankful this woman was his.

"You are so handsome," she murmured.

He touched his lips to hers. "And you are so beautiful. I love you."

"I love you, too."

Rillian felt the warmth move through him, amplified by the alien symbiont pulsing along his spine. He felt a tingle of answering energy from Dayna's symbiont.

His woman was so incredibly tough. She'd survived things that should have killed her, and had still come up ready to embrace life.

He wrapped an arm around her, scanning the party. His gaze fell on Galen and Sam. He watched the imperator tuck a strand of Sam's hair back behind her ear. The pair was lost in each other, oblivious to the party going on around them.

"I'm happy for him," Rillian said. "For them both."

"I'm happy for all of us," Dayna said. "Our abduction could have turned out very differently." She cupped Rillian's cheek. "I consider myself *very* lucky."

Everyone hated the Thraxians and all they'd done, but Rillian knew that the aliens had done one good thing —they'd brought these people from Earth into their lives. He was well aware that his entire existence was better because of Dayna.

She leaned into him. "Want to go home and get naked?"

Rillian smiled. "Always."

Magnus

MAGNUS HELD the sleeping child in the crook of his arm. *His* child.

Ever pressed into his side, and he was once again blindsided by how his life had changed. Changed beyond his wildest imaginings.

One day, he'd been an unfeeling cyborg imperator, and the next, a father with the woman he loved next to him.

He'd never believed that he could feel this much. *Love* this much.

Ever had changed everything. And baby Asha had changed it even more.

He counted Asha's eyelashes resting on her cheek. Then he listened to her quiet breaths. *Drak*, he was the father of this tiny little girl.

"You okay?" Ever stroked a hand down his arm.

"I love you."

Her lips quirked. "I know."

"I love her. I will do everything in my power to give you both everything you need."

A sweet look crossed her face. "We just need you to love us, Magnus. Everything else will fall into place."

He pressed his cheek to her dark hair, his baby a sweet weight in his arms. "I do. With everything I am."

"Imperator."

The voice of one of his elite cyborgs broke through the moment. Magnus focused on Toren, standing to attention beside them. "Yes, Toren?"

"Sorry to interrupt. Jax sent me with a priority message for you from an informant. I thought you'd want to see it."

Magnus had left his second-in-command, Jaxxer, in charge of the House of Rone for the evening. His cyborg best friend had always felt more deeply, and hadn't been happy to miss a party. Still, Magnus knew it wouldn't stop the man doing his job to the best of his ability.

Taking the paper, Magnus flicked it open. He read it and frowned. "Is it confirmed?"

"No. Just a rumor."

"Probability it is correct?"

"By my calculations, twenty-six-point-five percent."

Not high, but high enough that it couldn't be ignored. "Thank you, Toren. Please inform Jax to investigate this fully."

Toren nodded.

"And then get yourself a drink."

Toren blinked slowly. "A drink?"

"Yes, and join the party."

Magnus knew he would have had the same blank-faced expression as Toren's just a few months ago. As the cyborg turned to find himself a drink, Magnus saw Ever trying not to laugh. But when her gaze moved across his face, her smile faded.

"What's wrong?"

"Maybe nothing. I need to speak to Galen."

She nodded and took the sleeping baby out of his arms. "Go do your imperator thing." She pressed her cheek to his arm. "We'll be waiting."

A glow blossomed in his chest. Magnus felt the truth of her words and her love. She would always be there, waiting for him.

***

GALEN SAT ON A CHAIR, the party revolving around him, and Sam in his lap.

He was content and happy. *Drak*, it felt good. He nuzzled her neck, right where he'd bitten her. One day, if she allowed him, he'd mark her skin with ink to show his commitment.

"I want to help out with training the new gladiator recruits," Sam said.

Galen smiled. "They're your recruits."

She frowned. "What do you mean, they're my recruits?"

"Sam, you're mine. I love you."

Her gaze softened. "I know, boss-man."

"That means that what's mine is yours. The House of Galen is yours too."

She blinked. "Uh, wow. Okay." She tilted her head. "Does that mean I can be called Imperatoress?"

Galen laughed. "Only when you're in bed with me."

"I think I might like to fight in the arena, too. When I'm ready."

He stroked a hand down her arm. "Whatever you want." He loved watching her fight.

For the first time ever, Galen looked to the future with pure excitement. Not just to ensuring Raiden had what he needed, or that his people were safe and cared for, or that the innocent were rescued. For the first time, he considered all the things *he* wanted for himself, and they all revolved around the woman in his arms.

"Galen."

He looked up at Magnus and frowned. "Magnus. Problem?" He felt Sam stiffen.

"Probably nothing." The cyborg sat in a chair beside them. "I have an unconfirmed rumor to inform you about." He held up a folded note.

Instincts firing, Galen took the paper and opened it.

"What is it?" Sam peered at the alien script, but he knew she couldn't read it.

The words made Galen's fingers clench on the paper. "An unconfirmed rumor that the Thraxians had a small scout ship with them when they attacked Fortuna Station."

Sam sucked in a breath, her gaze zeroing in on his face. "And?"

"The main Thraxian ship was already almost at

capacity when they attacked Fortuna. That's why so few of you were taken."

Sam waited, her dark eyes intense.

"But the scout ship had space. There may be more abducted humans who were taken."

Her jaw tightened. "And they're here on Carthago? In captivity?"

"At this time, it's just a rumor," Magnus said. "We've calculated a twenty-six-point-five percent probability that it's correct."

Galen looked at his fellow imperator. "We all read the Thraxian manifest. Every single one of the humans listed in there is standing right here in the House of Galen."

Magnus nodded. "I am aware. However, I've already instructed Jaxxer to track this down and corroborate."

"You'll keep us informed," Galen demanded.

Magnus inclined his head. "Of course."

"Thank you, Magnus," Sam said.

As the cyborg walked away, Galen wrapped his arms around Sam. "Are you okay?"

She nodded. "I don't want to borrow trouble or worry the others. This might be nothing."

"Let's agree to wait and see what Magnus' cyborgs uncover."

"I pray it isn't true."

Suddenly, fireworks exploded into the sky. The partygoers cheered. Galen recognized Lore's handiwork when he saw it.

"But if there *are* more humans out there..." Sam's voice drifted off.

"We won't abandon them." He made a vow to himself that together they'd help find any other humans who might be out there. *If* they existed.

She smiled. "For honor and freedom, my noble imperator."

"For honor and freedom, my gorgeous partner, lover, champion."

He leaned down, pressing his mouth to hers, drinking deeply. As love filled him, his tattoos glowed, and he kept kissing her as more fireworks exploded overhead.

I hope you enjoyed Galen and Sam's story!

We haven't seen the last of Carthago and the House of Galen gladiators yet. Stay tuned for a novella set on the Corsair Caravan as part of the *Pets in Space Anthology* in October, starring Corsair's right-hands Mersi and Bren.

And look out for more in 2019:

HOUSE OF RONE

AND I have other exciting news for sci-fi romance lovers...I'll have the first book in a *brand-new* series coming at the end of 2018. Keep an eye out for **Eon Warriors** and the first book, *Edge of Eon*, where a wrongly-imprisoned space marine's only chance at freedom depends on her abducting a fearsome alien war commander.

For more action-packed romance, read on for a preview of the first chapter of *Marcus,* the first book in my best-selling Hell Squad series.

Don't miss out! For updates about new releases, action romance info, free books, and other fun stuff, sign up for my VIP mailing list and get your *free box set* containing three action-packed romances.

Visit here to get started: www.annahackettbooks.com

FREE BOX SET DOWNLOAD

JOIN THE ACTION-PACKED ADVENTURE!

PREVIEW - HELL SQUAD: MARCUS

READY FOR ANOTHER?

IN THE AFTERMATH OF AN ALIEN INVASION:

**HEROES WILL RISE...
WHEN THEY HAVE
SOMEONE TO LIVE FOR**

Her team was under attack.

Elle Milton pressed her fingers to her small earpiece. "Squad Six, you have seven more raptors inbound from the east." Her other hand gripped the edge of her comp screen, showing the enhanced drone feed.

She watched, her belly tight, as seven glowing red dots converged on the blue ones huddled together in the burned-out ruin of an office building in downtown

Sydney. Each blue dot was a squad member and one of them was their leader.

"Marcus? Do you copy?" Elle fought to keep her voice calm. No way she'd let them hear her alarm.

"Roger that, Elle." Marcus' gravelly voice filled her ear. Along with the roar of laser fire. "We see them."

She sagged back in her chair. This was the worst part. Just sitting there knowing that Marcus and the others were fighting for their lives. In the six months she'd been comms officer for the squad, she'd worked hard to learn the ropes. But there were days she wished she was out there, aiming a gun and taking out as many alien raptors as she could.

You're not a soldier, Ellianna. No, she was a useless party-girl-turned-survivor. She watched as a red dot disappeared off the screen, then another, and another. She finally drew a breath. Marcus and his team were the experienced soldiers. She'd just be a big fat liability in the field.

But she was a damn good comms officer.

Just then, a new cluster of red dots appeared near the team. She tapped the screen, took a measurement. "Marcus! More raptors are en route. They're about one kilometer away. North." God, would these invading aliens ever leave them alone?

"Shit," Marcus bit out. Then he went silent.

She didn't know if he was thinking or fighting. She pictured his rugged, scarred face creased in thought as he formulated a plan.

Then his deep, rasping voice was back. "Elle, we need an escape route and an evac now. Shaw's been hit in the leg, Cruz is carrying him. We can't engage more raptors."

She tapped the screen rapidly, pulling up drone images and archived maps. *Escape route, escape route.* Her mind clicked through the options. She knew Shaw was taller and heavier than Cruz, but the armor they wore had slim-line exoskeletons built into them allowing the soldiers to lift heavier loads and run faster and longer than normal. She tapped the screen again. *Come on.* She needed somewhere safe for a Hawk quadcopter to set down and pick them up.

"Elle? We need it now!"

Just then her comp beeped. She looked at the image and saw a hazy patch of red appear in the broken shell of a nearby building. The heat sensor had detected something else down there. Something big.

Right next to the team.

She touched her ear. "Rex! Marcus, a rex has just woken up in the building beside you."

"Fuck! Get us out of here. Now."

Oh, God. Elle swallowed back bile. Images of rexes, with their huge, dinosaur-like bodies and mouths full of teeth, flashed in her head.

More laser fire ripped through her earpiece and she heard the wild roar of the awakening beast.

Block it out. She focused on the screen. Marcus needed her. The team needed her.

"Run past the rex." One hand curled into a tight fist, her nails cutting into her skin. "Go through its hiding place."

"Through its nest?" Marcus' voice was incredulous. "You know how territorial they are."

"It's the best way out. On the other side you'll find a railway tunnel. Head south along it about eight hundred meters, and you'll find an emergency exit ladder that you can take to the surface. I'll have a Hawk pick you up there."

A harsh expulsion of breath. "Okay, Elle. You've gotten us out of too many tight spots for me to doubt you now."

His words had heat creeping into her cheeks. His praise...it left her giddy. In her life BAI—before alien invasion—no one had valued her opinions. Her father, her mother, even her almost-fiancé, they'd all thought her nothing more than a pretty ornament. Hell, she *had* been a silly, pretty party girl.

And because she'd been inept, her parents were dead. Elle swallowed. A year had passed since that horrible night during the first wave of the alien attack, when their giant ships had appeared in the skies. Her parents had died that night, along with most of the world.

"Hell Squad, ready to go to hell?" Marcus called out.

"Hell, yeah!" the team responded. "The devil needs an ass-kicking!"

"Woo-hoo!" Another voice blasted through her headset, pulling her from the past. "Ellie, baby, this dirty alien's nest stinks like Cruz's socks. You should be here."

A smile tugged at Elle's lips. Shaw Baird always knew how to ease the tension of a life-or-death situation.

"Oh, yeah, Hell Squad gets the best missions," Shaw added.

Elle watched the screen, her smile slipping. Everyone called Squad Six the Hell Squad. She was never quite sure if it was because they were hellions, or because they got sent into hell to do the toughest, dirtiest missions.

There was no doubt they were a bunch of rebels. Marcus had a rep for not following orders. Just the previous week, he'd led the squad in to destroy a raptor outpost but had detoured to rescue survivors huddled in an abandoned hospital that was under attack. At the debrief, the general's yelling had echoed through the entire base. Marcus, as always, had been silent.

"Shut up, Shaw, you moron." The deep female voice carried an edge.

Elle had decided there were two words that best described the only female soldier on Hell Squad—loner and tough. Claudia Frost was everything Elle wasn't. Elle cleared her throat. "Just get yourselves back to base."

As she listened to the team fight their way through the rex nest, she tapped in the command for one of the Hawk quadcopters to pick them up.

The line crackled. "Okay, Elle, we're through. Heading to the evac point."

Marcus' deep voice flowed over her and the tense muscles in her shoulders relaxed a fraction. They'd be back soon. They were okay. He was okay.

She pressed a finger to the blue dot leading the team. "The bird's en route, Marcus."

"Thanks. See you soon."

She watched on the screen as the large, black shadow of the Hawk hovered above the ground and the team boarded. The rex was headed in their direction, but they were already in the air.

Elle stood and ran her hands down her trousers. She shot a wry smile at the camouflage fabric. It felt like a dream to think that she'd ever owned a very expensive, designer wardrobe. And heels—God, how long had it been since she'd worn heels? These days, fatigues were all that hung in her closet. Well-worn ones, at that.

As she headed through the tunnels of the underground base toward the landing pads, she forced herself not to run. She'd see him—them—soon enough. She rounded a corner and almost collided with someone.

"General. Sorry, I wasn't watching where I was going."

"No problem, Elle." General Adam Holmes had a military-straight bearing he'd developed in the United Coalition Army and a head of dark hair with a brush of distinguished gray at his temples. He was classically handsome, and his eyes were a piercing blue. He was the top man in this last little outpost of humanity. "Squad Six on their way back?"

"Yes, sir." They fell into step.

"And they secured the map?"

God, Elle had almost forgotten about the map. "Ah, yes. They got images of it just before they came under attack by raptors."

"Well, let's go welcome them home. That map might just be the key to the fate of mankind."

They stepped into the landing areas. Staff in various military uniforms and civilian clothes raced around. After the raptors had attacked, bringing all manner of vicious creatures with them to take over the Earth, what was left of mankind had banded together.

Whoever had survived now lived here in an underground base in the Blue Mountains, just west of Sydney, or in the other, similar outposts scattered across the planet. All arms of the United Coalition's military had been decimated. In the early days, many of the surviving soldiers had fought amongst themselves, trying to work out who outranked whom. But it didn't take long before General Holmes had unified everyone against the aliens. Most squads were a mix of ranks and experience, but the teams eventually worked themselves out. Most didn't even bother with titles and rank anymore.

Sirens blared, followed by the clang of metal. Huge doors overhead retracted into the roof.

A Hawk filled the opening, with its sleek gray body and four spinning rotors. It was near-silent, running on a small thermonuclear engine. It turned slowly as it descended to the landing pad.

Her team was home.

She threaded her hands together, her heart beating a little faster.

Marcus was home.

Marcus Steele wanted a shower and a beer.

Hot, sweaty and covered in raptor blood, he leaped down from the Hawk and waved at his team to follow. He kept a sharp eye on the medical team who raced out to tend to Shaw. Dr. Emerson Green was leading them, her white lab coat snapping around her curvy body. The blonde doctor caught his gaze and tossed him a salute.

Shaw was cursing and waving them off, but one look from Marcus and the lanky Australian sniper shut his mouth.

Marcus swung his laser carbine over his shoulder and scraped a hand down his face. Man, he'd kill for a hot shower. Of course, he'd have to settle for a cold one since they only allowed hot water for two hours in the morning in order to conserve energy. But maybe after that beer he'd feel human again.

"Well done, Squad Six." Holmes stepped forward. "Steele, I hear you got images of the map."

Holmes might piss Marcus off sometimes, but at least the guy always got straight to the point. He was a general to the bone and always looked spit and polish. Everything about him screamed money and a fancy education, so not surprisingly, he tended to rub the troops the wrong way.

Marcus pulled the small, clear comp chip from his pocket. "We got it."

Then he spotted her.

Shit. It was always a small kick in his chest. His gaze traveled up Elle Milton's slim figure, coming to rest on a face he could stare at all day. She wasn't very tall, but that didn't matter. Something about her high cheekbones, pale-blue eyes, full lips, and rain of chocolate-brown hair...it all worked for him. Perfectly. She was beautiful, kind, and far too good to be stuck in this crappy underground maze of tunnels, dressed in hand-me-down fatigues.

She raised a slim hand. Marcus shot her a small nod.

"Hey, Ellie-girl. Gonna give me a kiss?"

Shaw passed on an iono-stretcher hovering off the ground and Marcus gritted his teeth. The tall, blond sniper with his lazy charm and Aussie drawl was popular with the ladies. Shaw flashed his killer smile at Elle.

She smiled back, her blue eyes twinkling and Marcus' gut cramped.

Then she put one hand on her hip and gave the sniper a head-to-toe look. She shook her head. "I think you get enough kisses."

Marcus released the breath he didn't realize he was holding.

"See you later, Sarge." Zeke Jackson slapped Marcus on the back and strolled past. His usually-silent twin, Gabe, was beside him. The twins, both former Coalition Army Special Forces soldiers, were deadly in the field. Marcus was damned happy to have them on his squad.

"Howdy, Princess." Claudia shot Elle a smirk as she passed.

Elle rolled her eyes. "Claudia."

Cruz, Marcus' second-in-command and best friend from their days as Coalition Marines, stepped up beside Marcus and crossed his arms over his chest. He'd already pulled some of his lightweight body armor off, and the ink on his arms was on display.

The general nodded at Cruz before looking back at Marcus. "We need Shaw back up and running ASAP. If the raptor prisoner we interrogated is correct, that map shows one of the main raptor communications hubs." There was a blaze of excitement in the usually-stoic general's voice. "It links all their operations together."

Yeah, Marcus knew it was big. Destroy the hub, send the raptor operations into disarray.

The general continued. "As soon as the tech team can break the encryption on the chip and give us a location for the raptor comms hub—" his piercing gaze leveled on Marcus "—I want your team back out there to plant the bomb."

Marcus nodded. He knew if they destroyed the raptors' communications it gave humanity a fighting chance. A chance they desperately needed.

He traded a look with Cruz. Looked like they were going out to wade through raptor gore again sooner than anticipated.

Man, he really wanted that beer.

Then Marcus' gaze landed on Elle again. He didn't keep going out there for himself, or Holmes. He went so people like Elle and the other civilian survivors had a chance. A chance to do more than simply survive.

"Shaw's wound is minor. Doc Emerson should have him good as new in an hour or so." Since the advent of the nano-meds, simple wounds could be healed in hours, rather than days and weeks. They carried a dose of the microscopic medical machines on every mission, but only for dire emergencies. The nano-meds had to be administered and monitored by professionals or they were just as likely to kill you from the inside than heal you.

General Holmes nodded. "Good."

Elle cleared her throat. "There's no telling how long it will take to break the encryption. I've been working with the tech team and even if they break it, we may not be able to translate it all. We're getting better at learning the raptor language but there are still huge amounts of it we don't yet understand."

Marcus' jaw tightened. There was always something. He knew Noah Kim—their resident genius computer specialist—and his geeks were good, but if they couldn't read the damn raptor language...

Holmes turned. "Steele, let your team have some downtime and be ready the minute Noah has anything."

"Yes, sir." As the general left, Marcus turned to Cruz. "Go get yourself a beer, Ramos."

"Don't need to tell me more than once, *amigo*. I would kill for some of my dad's tamales to go with it." Something sad flashed across a face all the women in the base mooned over, then he grimaced and a bone-deep weariness colored his words. "Need to wash the raptor off me, first." He tossed Marcus a casual salute, Elle a smile, and strode out.

Marcus frowned after his friend and absently started loosening his body armor.

Elle moved up beside him. "I can take the comp chip to Noah."

"Sure." He handed it to her. When her fingers brushed his he felt the warmth all the way through him. Hell, he had it bad. Thankfully, he still had his armor on or she'd see his cock tenting his pants.

"I'll come find you as soon as we have something." She glanced up at him. Smiled. "Are you going to rec night tonight? I hear Cruz might even play guitar for us."

The Friday-night gathering was a chance for everyone to blow off a bit of steam and drink too much homebrewed beer. And Cruz had an unreal talent with a guitar, although lately Marcus hadn't seen the man play too much.

Marcus usually made an appearance at these parties, then left early to head back to his room to study raptor movements or plan the squad's next missions. "Yeah, I'll be there."

"Great." She smiled. "I'll see you there, then." She hurried out clutching the chip.

He stared at the tunnel where she'd exited for a long while after she disappeared, and finally ripped his chest armor off. Ah, on second thought, maybe going to the rec night wasn't a great idea. Watching her pretty face and captivating smile would drive him crazy. He cursed under his breath. He really needed that cold shower.

As he left the landing pads, he reminded himself he should be thinking of the mission. Destroy the hub and kill more aliens. Rinse and repeat. Death and killing, that was about all he knew.

He breathed in and caught a faint trace of Elle's floral scent. She was clean and fresh and good. She always worried about them, always had a smile, and she was damned good at providing their comms and intel.

She was why he fought through the muck every day. So she could live and the goodness in her would survive. She deserved more than blood and death and killing.

And she sure as hell deserved more than a battled-scarred, bloodstained soldier.

Hell Squad
Marcus
Cruz

Gabe
Reed
Roth
Noah
Shaw
Holmes
Niko
Finn
Theron
Hemi
Ash
Levi
Manu
Also Available as Audiobooks!

PREVIEW - AMONG GALACTIC RUINS

MORE ACTION ROMANCE?

**ACTION
ADVENTURE
TREASURE HUNTS
SEXY SCI-FI ROMANCE**

When astro-archeologist and museum curator Dr. Lexa Carter discovers a secret map to a lost old Earth treasure— a priceless Fabergé egg—she's excited at the prospect of a treasure hunt to the dangerous desert planet of Zerzura. What she's not so happy about is being saddled with a bodyguard—the museum's mysterious new head of security, Damon Malik.

After many dangerous years as a galactic spy, Damon

Malik just wanted a quiet job where no one tried to kill him. Instead of easy work in a museum full of artifacts, he finds himself on a backwater planet babysitting the most infuriating woman he's ever met.

She thinks he's arrogant. He thinks she's a trouble-magnet. But among the desert sands and ruins, adventure led by a young, brash treasure hunter named Dathan Phoenix, takes a deadly turn. As it becomes clear that someone doesn't want them to find the treasure, Lexa and Damon will have to trust each other just to survive.

The Phoenix Adventures

Among Galactic Ruins
At Star's End
In the Devil's Nebula
On a Rogue Planet
Beneath a Trojan Moon
Beyond Galaxy's Edge
On a Cyborg Planet
Return to Dark Earth
On a Barbarian World
Lost in Barbarian Space
Through Uncharted Space
Crashed on an Ice World

ALSO BY ANNA HACKETT

Treasure Hunter Security

Undiscovered

Uncharted

Unexplored

Unfathomed

Untraveled

Unmapped

Unidentified

Undetected

Galactic Gladiators

Gladiator

Warrior

Hero

Protector

Champion

Barbarian

Beast

Rogue

Guardian

Cyborg

Imperator

Also Available as Audiobooks!

Hell Squad

Marcus

Cruz

Gabe

Reed

Roth

Noah

Shaw

Holmes

Niko

Finn

Theron

Hemi

Ash

Levi

Manu

Also Available as Audiobooks!

The Anomaly Series

Time Thief

Mind Raider

Soul Stealer

Salvation

Anomaly Series Box Set

The Phoenix Adventures

Among Galactic Ruins

At Star's End

In the Devil's Nebula

On a Rogue Planet

Beneath a Trojan Moon

Beyond Galaxy's Edge

On a Cyborg Planet

Return to Dark Earth

On a Barbarian World

Lost in Barbarian Space

Through Uncharted Space

Crashed on an Ice World

Perma Series

Winter Fusion

A Galactic Holiday

Warriors of the Wind

Tempest

Storm & Seduction

Fury & Darkness

Standalone Titles

Savage Dragon

Hunter's Surrender

One Night with the Wolf

For more information visit AnnaHackettBooks.com

ABOUT THE AUTHOR

I'm a USA Today bestselling author and I'm passionate about ***action romance***. I love stories that combine the thrill of falling in love with the excitement of action, danger and adventure. I'm a sucker for that moment when the team is walking in slow motion, shoulder-to-shoulder heading off into battle. I write about people overcoming unbeatable odds and achieving seemingly impossible goals. I like to believe it's possible for all of us to do the same.

My books are mixture of action, adventure and sexy romance and they're recommended for anyone who enjoys fast-paced stories where the boy wins the girl at the end (or sometimes the girl wins the boy!)

For release dates, action romance info, free books, and other fun stuff, sign up for the latest news here:

Website: www.annahackettbooks.com

Lightning Source UK Ltd.
Milton Keynes UK
UKHW011908050719
345651UK00001B/22/P

9 781925 539554